Kissed
By A
Hood Prince

BIANCA MARIE

SULLIVAN
PRODUCTIONS
LITERARY&FILMS

www.leosullivanpresents.com

© 2018
Published by Leo Sullivan Presents
www.leolsullivan.com

This book is dedicated to my children, Ahmir and Alanna. I love you guys so much!! Everything I do, I do it for y'all! You two inspire me to be great, and I promise I'm not gonna stop grinding until we get where we need to be. I love you, my babies!

A MESSAGE TO BIANCA'S BOMB ASS READERS!!!

I love you guys so much! This is book number 24 for me, and I just wanna thank you guys for always rocking with me. Sometimes the journey is a rough one, but it's because of you guys that I keep pushing to keep producing some fire from my pen. I'm so happy that you guys enjoy everything I come with. I'm extremely grateful for my readers. I wouldn't be where I'm at today in this industry without the love from the readers. So, thank you!! I appreciate you all for rocking with me.

Xoxo_ Bianca Marie

ABOUT THE AUTHOR

Want to Know More about Bianca Marie?
Stay Updated

Add me on Facebook my main page @ Bianca Marie
Add my second Facebook page @ Authoress Bianca Marie
For sneak peeks, contests, and more join my reader's group
on Facebook
@Bianca's Bookaholic's
Follow me on Instagram @ Biancamariebookz87
Follow me on Twitter @ BiancaBooks16

THE PRESENT...

As I stood at the podium and looked at the onlookers in the crowd, my heart rate sped up. This was the first time I had ever done something like this, but it needed to be done. I needed to be an advocate for all those girls out there like me. Those girls who didn't have a voice, girls who endured bullying, abuse, and mistreatment from those they loved. Today, I would be that voice. Maybe my story could reach and touch others. Hopefully, it could make a difference.

"My name is Kimora Eldredge, and I'm the owner of S.W.A.G., and as you all know, it means Saving Women and Girls. I'm more than honored to have all of you here. My program was created to help empower women. Most of you don't know me because I chose to remain anonymous. I never wanted people to know my truth, but just like you, I have a story too. The diamonds in my ear, the rings on my finger, and the Gucci bag I'm carrying, I didn't always have.

I was a victim of abuse, I was a victim of heartbreak. Just a victim altogether. But I became stronger, wiser, and I've grown into a better person.

"Before I could get to that, I did some childish things, things I could've prevented, and I did some dumb things in my life, but today I choose to live in my truth. No more hiding, no more secrets…"

I stopped midsentence when I looked up and stared into the audience. My eyes roamed the crowd, and I got choked up when I saw a familiar pair of eyes staring back into mine. His arms were folded across his chest, and he was sporting a crisp, white polo shirt and dark, denim jeans. His curly hair was trimmed up nicely on the sides, and his thin goatee had him looking sexy as all hell. A year had passed since I walked away from him, but the feelings never left. My heart rate increased, and my mouth dried. I swallowed hard and exhaled.

"I'm not perfect, and my life wasn't grand. Life was a struggle for me. I've been fighting all my life, fighting for happiness, for respect, and for love. I got to the point where I was tired of fighting." My eyes landed on him.

"Today, I'm gonna tell you a story about a girl whose life changed drastically, and the day she kissed a Hood Prince, she knew she would forever be changed," I spoke into the mic and exhaled before I started my trek down memory lane.

The memories
from way back when...

THIS NIGHTMARE CALLED LIFE

KIMORA

"**G**et cho' fat ass up out that fucking bed! You sloppy ass bitch!" my step mother, Candice, yelled at me.

I sat up in bed and let out a deep sigh. When I looked over at my bedroom door, Candice was standing there mean mugging the hell out of me.

"I'm up!" I said in a low tone, still sitting on the edge of my bed.

"Well, I can't fucking tell. You still sitting there, fat ass. Get cho ass up and move. Breakfast is ready, and I know you wanna feed yo fat ass face before you walk out of the door," she spat and slammed my bedroom door.

I shook my head but didn't say anything in response to her. I never said anything. Truthfully, I didn't even have the courage to get up and go to school. I was sick and tired of it. I hated the school and those people who went there.

My father was in the army, and when he was away, I was stuck with his crazy ass wife. My mother, Laya, died when I was nine years old, and that's when he met this monster. I was irritated to the max. Some days, I didn't even wanna get out of bed. I hated school. This was my last year, and I couldn't wait to graduate.

I pulled myself out the bed and headed for the bathroom. As I looked myself over in the mirror, I was disgusted by what I saw. My Name is Kimora Eldredge, and I was 195 pounds of insecurity, and I hated who I was. I hated having dark skin, and my long hair didn't do any justice for me. I got teased all the fucking time. Between my peers at school and my home life, it was so fucking hard for me on a daily basis to just even survive.

Tears slid down my face as I thought about another day of fucking torture that I would endure. I hated everyone at my school. I hated my neighborhood; I just hated my life. A knock on the bathroom door startled me out of my thoughts.

"Yes?" I shouted.

"Mora, hurry up! I gotta piss," my twin brother, Knox, yelled through the door.

"Okay, I'm coming!"

I grabbed my face towel and washed my face then opened the door. For me and Knox to be twins, we were total opposites. He was muscle bound from being on the football team. My brother didn't look like your average eighteen-year-old. He could have passed for more like twenty-one or something.

"Morning, sis." He smiled at me and pinched my chin.

"Mornin' Bruh Bruh," I said and walked out of the bathroom.

Knox was the only one who had my back. I couldn't tell you throughout our course of high school how many people he had beat up for messing with me. Now, I didn't tell him what was going on because I just needed to handle my own shit.

I went to my bedroom and proceeded to get dressed for the day. I didn't even wash my ass. Hell, I didn't even care. Nobody fucked with me at school anyway. I had no fucking friends or dudes who even looked my way.

After dressing, I descended the stairs and walked into the kitchen. My little brother, Kade, was sitting at the breakfast table, and so was Candice's son, Trey. Trey wasn't my brother, and I couldn't stand his bitch ass either. I wouldn't dare say that aloud, though. He was seventeen years old, just a year older than Kade.

I grabbed a bagel and put some eggs on my plate then sat down at the table. I ate my food slowly only looking down. I wouldn't make eye contact with Trey because if I did, he was gonna start up his morning shenanigans.

"What's up, fat ass?" He snickered.

I looked up and rolled my eyes, but I didn't say anything in response to his ass. I knew it was just best to ignore him. Kade looked at me and slightly smiled. My little brother was such a follower. He worshipped the ground Trey walked on, and it was utterly disgusting in my eyes. He was my brother, but he acted as if I wasn't his sister. He would crack jokes about me right along with Trey.

"Bitch, yo' fat ass ain't hear me speak to you?" he barked, and I looked up at him in my face.

"Leave me alone, Trey," I uttered.

"Nah, that shit is rude. Fat ass, speak to me!" he roared, and I exhaled deeply.

See what I was talking about? This dude acted as if he hated me, and I didn't do shit to him.

"Muthafucka, call my sister out of her name again, and I'm gon' break ya fucking jaw." Knox's voice came out of nowhere.

I turned around, and he was standing behind me. I slightly smiled, and he winked his eye at me.

"K... I... I was only fucking around with her," he stuttered

"Nah, nigga, don't fucking play with her. She ain't a fucking toy. And I ain't gon' tell you that shit again."

"K... I ain't mean—"

"Nah, nigga, you meant that shit! Let me hear you say some foul ass shit to my sister again, and Imma fuck you up, nigga. Now YOU speak to her, bitch ass nigga!" Knox barked, and Trey's eyes got big as saucers.

"Goo... good morning, Kimora," Trey stuttered, and I smirked.

I loved my brother because he always had my back. That's what Trey's punk ass gets.

"That's what the fuck I thought, nigga," Knox growled as he stared down at him.

"Hey! Hey now! Knox, watch your mouth in my house," Candice scolded, coming into the kitchen with a frown on her face.

"What? Man, get cho bitch ass on." K sneered.

"I'm not gonna tell you again to watch your mouth in my house, and don't call my son out of his name. He's your brother too, whether you wanna believe it or not," Candice snapped.

"That nigga ain't my fucking brother, fuck him. And fuck this house. This ain't yo house, this my momma house," Knox snapped and walked out the back door.

Candice mugged me like it was my fault.

"Kimora, you're always starting trouble. Ole sloppy ass. Hurry up and get out of this house and get cho fat ass to school," she snapped.

I looked at her and I didn't say anything. I didn't even want the eggs anymore, so I pushed away from the table, got up, and walked out the back door. When I got outside and looked around for Knox, he wasn't waiting for me, so I headed for the bus stop. I was low key mad that K left me. We usually walked to school together. He was pissed the fuck off. Knox couldn't stand Candice just as much as I couldn't. It had to be a twin thing.

When my daddy met Candice, I was ten years old. He's been with her ever since. My father, Captain Louis Eldredge, was always gone, shipped out overseas. And we were always stuck with the fucking stepmother from hell. When my momma died, that's when I started overeating. I missed my momma something terrible. She was a beautiful woman whose smile lit up the room when she came inside. It was something about her aura that brought a smile to everyone's face.

I've been miserable ever since she left. My daddy was a

good man, but the bitch Candice was a horrible person. He just didn't know the woman he married. She was a fucking monster. No one knew what I endured behind the closed doors of our home. Not her church going ass friends, not my Daddy, not my teachers, no one. I was all alone. I don't know why I endured this bullshit when all I had to do was say something, but I couldn't say anything because honestly, I feared her. I didn't think my father would have believed me anyway.

Waiting at the bus stop, nervousness ran through my body. I hoped and prayed like hell that I didn't see Sierra and her crew. Sierra was a bitch who thought she was the toughest of the school. She fucked with me on a daily basis, and there was nothing I could do about it. I avoided her like hell every chance I got.

The bus pulled up, and I got on. My mind wandered as I rode the bus. I didn't have a clue what I was going to do with my life after high school. All I knew was that I was ready for it to be over.

When I got off the bus in front of John Hope High School, I exhaled deeply. I walked across the street and standing right there in front of the school was Sierra and her crew of friends.

"Look at this fat ass knock kneed bitch," Sierra spewed, causing snickers from her friends.

I hung my head low as I tried to walk around her and her crew, but she stepped in front of me.

"Kimora, Kimora, Kimora," she spoke my name, and I looked up at her.

She was beautiful. Light skinned with freckles around

her nose, and she had long hair that hung down her back. She was slender, and she had enticing hazel eyes. Overall, she was something that I would never be.

"Just leave me alone, Sierra," I said with my head down as I tried to go around her.

She wouldn't let me. "What, chu scared or something, bitch?" she taunted, and I still refused to respond.

I didn't have time for Sierra and her shit. She did this to me all the fucking time, and I was sick and fucking tired of it.

"Leave me alone, Sierra!" I shouted as she pushed me.

"Or what? What cha gonna do, fat ass?" She laughed and pushed me again, causing me to fall to the ground.

I dropped my books as I scraped my knee. When I looked up, her and all her friends were laughing. Tears welled up in my eyes as embarrassment took over.

"Ohhhh, Porky Pig is gonna cry," she taunted as I stood up on wobbly legs.

Before I could walk off, someone bum rushed the crowd.

"Get the fuck away from sister, shawty," Knox's deep voice boomed through the crowd. He stepped forward, and a smile appeared on my face.

"Or what, bitch ass nigga? Fuck this fat bitch."

Sierra laughed, and out the blue, Knox smacked the shit out of her. I heard gasps and, "Oh my god, he just slapped Sierra"

"Aye, bro! Aye, bro!" this dude named Prince said as he grabbed Knox up and pulled him away.

Sierra was hollering and screaming, talking about how she was gonna get him fucked up.

I happily wiped my tears and walked off.

This was life for me on a daily basis except for the part about Knox smacking Sierra. That was a first. He's never hit a girl before.

Once in the school, I went to my first class and got my day started. It was crazy how drama always followed me, and I never did anything to anybody.

PROTECTING MY FAMILY WITH EVERYTHING IN ME

KNOX

"**M**an, what the fuck, bro? You can't be smacking bitches like that," my nigga, Prince, said to me as we walked around the back of the school.

I didn't even go inside. I was already having a bad fucking day due to my bitch ass stepmother who I couldn't fucking stand. And I couldn't stand her clown ass son either. The bitch was always talking shit to Kimora. Everybody was always fucking with Kimora.

"I'm sick of that bitch Sierra, bro. She better quit fucking with my sister," I said in a matter of fact tone.

"Nigga, you know her brother is from the low end, and he's a GD."

"Nigga, Ion give a fuck about no gangs. I ain't with that shit, but I can hold my own. I ain't some bitch ass nigga. My pops ain't raise me to be that way."

"Nigga, I'm already knowing. Shit, I ain't worried about it either. I'm just saying, we gon' have to be on point if the nigga slides up here. You know she gon' tell that bitch ass nigga," he stated, and I shrugged.

"Ion give a fuck. She can tell 'em. I'm gon' smack shawty ass every time I see her fucking with my sister. I'm tired of these hoes fucking with twin, bruh," I said, calling Kimora by the nickname we'd given each other. I called her twin at times, and she called me twin or Bruh Bruh.

"Yeah, I feel that shit, nigga. You already know, you ride I ride."

"That's why you my nigga." I smirked and dapped him up

"But, aye, you think Coach gon' find out? You know if he does, they gon' suspend you, and you ain't gon be able to play."

"Man, fuck this school. Fuck Coach, fuck that bitch, Sierra, fuck everybody. Today ain't my day, bruh, and any muthafucka can catch this shit," I expressed.

I was irritated. All I wanted was to have a conversation with my pops. Damn, I missed my pops and my momma. Shit hadn't been right since the day my moms left this earth. I think about her on a daily basis. I hated that Mora had so little self-esteem. She was beautiful, and I wished she could see it. She looked just like my momma. It was crazy.

I was a built ass nigga to be eighteen. Most muthafuckas thought I was twenty-one years old, but that wasn't the case. A nigga liked to work out. My nigga, Prince, had been the homie since freshmen year of high school and we were on the football team together. He was quarterback, and I was a wide receiver. Together, we made it happen on the field. A lot of times, I got compliments and shit from my teachers, saying that I would have a promising future in football if I just stuck to it. But that was hard to do with the lure of the streets calling me.

My little brother, Kade, was a fucking follower, and I hoped like hell he became his own man soon, or these fucking streets were gonna eat his ass up. As long as he had me, though, I was gonna make sure he's straight at all times.

Me and Prince sat on the bench behind the school, and he pulled out a blunt from in his pocket. He sparked it up and inhaled it deeply. Afterward, he passed it to me.

"Man, how yo big brother been doing?" I asked, speaking on his older brother, Terror.

He was way older than us and doing his thing in the streets.

"That nigga good. Shit, me and my moms don't hear from him that much." He shrugged, and I passed him the blunt back.

My cell vibrated in my back pocket, and when I pulled it out, I saw that it was this lil chick named Daisy. I met her a football game four months ago.

"Yooooo?" I answered.

"Hey boo." She giggled, and I smirked.

"What's good with you, ma?"

"Nothing much. My parents are gone to work, and I'm home alone. I wanted to see if you wanted to come over and chill with me for the day."

I frowned when she said that shit. I didn't like bitches

who weren't smart, and her not going to school was a dumb ass broad move to me.

"Nah, shawty. I'm about to head to class. Something yo ass should be doing. Don't hit my line no mo. I'll call you if I want my dick sucked," I spat and hung up the phone in her face.

"Aye, bruh, what the fuck you do that shit for? Yo ass crazy nigga." Prince laughed.

"Man, I can't stand dumb ass, dick seeking ass bitches."

"Nigga, shit, you better than me. I would've slid on shawty ass," Prince added.

"I know you would have. Ol' hot dick ass nigga. Yo ass gon' catch something, fucking all those lame ass broads."

"Whatever, nigga. I use a condom all the fucking time. I ain't worried."

"What's up with Spirit, though?" I asked, speaking of Spirit Meyers.

Shawty was everything a nigga was looking for. Most muthafuckas would've called her ass a bookworm or a nerd, but I loved the quiet as a mouse, church girl shit.

"Nigga, she cool. Stay away from Spirit. She doesn't need you corrupting her image," he joked, and I pushed him.

"Nigga, fuck you." I chuckled.

"Nah, man, she's a good girl, though. That's been my homie since the sand box. You gon' fuck up her life if she starts fucking with you," he said.

"Shit, nigga, I can change her life. You just don't fucking know." I laughed again.

Me and Prince chopped it up on the bench until it was time for the next class. When the bell rang, we both got up and walked into the school. I was a tough ass nigga, but I wasn't a dumb nigga. I went to school, and I made at least a C average in every fucking class. My pops was in the service, so he expected nothing but greatness from us.

Once we were in the school, we parted ways, each of us going to our classes. As I roamed the halls, I spotted my little brother, Kade. I walked up on him, and I could smell weed reeking off him. He didn't even see me because his back was turned to me.

"Aye, bro," I said, and he jumped then slightly turned around to face me.

"What's up, bro?" He smiled with his eyes low and the color of crimson red.

"Why the fuck you smell like weed?" I asked him in a low tone through gritted teeth.

"I was blowing with Trey. You already know," he said with a stupid ass grin on his face.

"Man, yo ass sound dumb as shit. Get the fuck out of here. You bet not ever be doing no dumb ass shit like that again. You think that shit is cool?"

"So, what? Nigga, you smoke," he snapped, and I got up on him.

"Nigga, I don't give a fuck what I do. Do better than me. The fuck is you doing? You following behind that lame ass nigga. Nigga gon' fuck around and get you killed out here while you being a follower and shit"

"You ain't my daddy, K... Fuck out of here."

"Nigga, I ain't gotta be ya daddy to fuck yo ass up in this hallway. Keep getting smart at the mouth," I snapped back, daring him to get tough with me.

I hated that follower the leader shit he was doing. Kade was smart as fuck, but he was too stupid to realize who the fuck he was. He wanted to be something he was not so bad, and that shit irked the fuck out of me.

"Man, aight." He huffed as he tried to walk around me,, but I stopped him because I instantly felt bad about talking to him like that. Kimora and Kade were my life, and I only wanted the best for them.

"Kade. Man, look…"

"I said aight, K. I heard you." He scoffed and walked away.

I hope he did hear me. That nigga Trey wasn't shit but trouble. Only if he knew, I can smell it. That's why I didn't like the lil nigga nor his moms.

After speaking to Kade, I went in my world history class and found my seat in the back of the class right behind Spirit.

Spirit Meyers was a nerd. She was chocolate, with long, wavy hair like she was mixed or some shit. She kept it brushed in a ponytail that hung down her back. Her cheekbones were high, and she had pearly, white teeth. Spirit wore black rimmed glasses, and her clothing usually consisted of jeans and t-shirts with a pair of sneakers. Baby girl was homely looking, but I loved that shit. She ain't have to wear a bunch of girly, skin tight clothes for me to notice her. She was gorgeous to me.

"Good morning, class. So, today I am going to assign a project on World War II. You will be partnered up in groups of two," our teacher, Ms. Lane announced. She went on to read off the paper who would be partnered up with who.

I couldn't help but glance over at Spirit who was sitting in front of me. Once she got to my name, my ears perked up to see who she would be partnering me up with.

"Knox and Spirit, you're gonna be partners," she announced.

A grin washed over my face. Just what I wanted.

"Class, go sit next to your partner and discuss some ideas. The project is due next week. I expect all of them to be done. No excuses," she said.

Spirit turned around and looked at me.

"You gonna come over here, or you want me to move next to you?" I asked her.

"I'll come back there," she replied in that sweet ass voice.

She got out her seat and sat next to me in the empty desk. I opened my notebook and stared at her.

"Why you looking at me like that?" she said in a low tone.

"I'm just looking. I can look, right?" I smiled, and she blushed.

"I guess you can look, Knox."

"Okay, so what ideas do you have?" she asked.

"I got an idea. See, I was thinking that... I wanna take you out," I said, and she laughed.

"Seriously, K, come on. Let's get to work."

"I am working... I'm working on this date," I joked again, but I was dead ass serious.

"Knox, I'm not about to be dealing with you. These hoes in the school are obsessed with you, and I don't think that I'm on your level."

"And why would you say that?"

"Because you're an athlete. You go after bitches who look like mini supermodels. Plus, Prince told me how you were."

When she said that shit, I frowned. Prince was my homie. I couldn't believe he was dissing me like that, and he knew I was feeling her.

"So that bitch ass nigga been talking shit about me?" I questioned with a frown on my face.

"Nooooo, he didn't say anything bad about you, but he did say something about you feeling me. I thought he was playing. I like you, Knox, but only as a friend. I have too much going on in my life, and my only focus is graduating."

"Well, it's true. I'm feeling you, shawty, and I want you to stop playing with a nigga and let me take you out, Spirit. I'm a good person. I ain't gon' bite yo ass unless you want me to," I told her, and she laughed.

"No, Knox. I think I'll pass. I just wanna finish school. Graduate, and go to college, that's it. Now come on and let's discuss some ideas," she suggested.

I decided to leave her alone for now. I would respect how she felt, but I was feeling Spirit like a muthafucka. Too much just to let her not fuck with a nigga.

ONCE SCHOOL WAS OVER, I MADE MY WAY THROUGH THE HALLS, and I couldn't get Spirit off my mind. When I got outside, I saw a large crowd formed, and everybody was running toward it to see what the fuck was going on. At first, I wasn't concerned with it because shit like this happened every day at this school, but then I heard Kimora's name, and that shit piqued my interest.

I raced over to the large crowd, and when I got right there, I saw a couple of niggas surrounding Kimora and Sierra while Sierra was stomping the shit out of my sister. I bum rushed the crowd and started swinging on niggas. First, I grabbed that bitch, Sierra, and tossed her ass to the side. Then I reached down, grabbed Mora's hand, and helped her off the ground. Her face was cut, and she was bleeding profusely. That shit made me angrier as I examined my sister's face.

While I was focused on Mora's face, I was hit in the back of the head. I turned around, and a big ass nigga who I knew was Sierra's brother was standing there with a bottle in his hand. Ole pancake ass nigga. The hit didn't even hurt me. I two pieced that bitch ass nigga with the quickness, and he stumbled backward. I got on top of his ass, but his homies started kicking me and shit. I wouldn't let up as I began to beat the shit out of the nigga.

One of the bitch ass niggas was able to pull me off dude, and I fell on my back. They started swinging on me, and out the corner of my eye, I spotted a brick lying next to me. I picked that muthafucka up and swung it as hard as I could, knocking that bitch ass nigga clean the fuck out.

Once he was off me, I got up and jumped on top of him, steadily beating him with the brick until he was unconscious. I was in a zone when I was on top of dude, and I didn't know what or who stopped me. By the time the shit was over, I was in handcuffs and being led to the back of a squad car. Damn, man.

Once I was in the back of the police cruiser, I leaned my head back against the seat. I exhaled deeply as I thought about my predicament. Shit wasn't looking good for me at all, and I knew I wouldn't be there to protect Kimora anymore. The squad car pulled off, and I looked out the window as all my peers stood around staring at me. Honestly, I didn't give a fuck about none of them mutha-fuckas in that crowd but one person.

I locked eyes with Spirit, and she had a sad look on her face. Damn, I fucked up this time, and I hoped like hell I ain't kill the nigga. If I did, I knew was going away for fucking murder.

NO ONE KNOWS MY PAIN

SPIRIT

As I got off the bus on 55th and Aberdeen, I couldn't get Knox off my mind. I tried to play hard to get with him when he asked me out on a date because I knew deep down inside, I was no match for him. Now that the shit had happened at the school, I hoped like hell he's okay. I hoped he doesn't have to be in jail for a long period of time because he was just trying to help his sister.

I knew who Kimora was. We weren't friends, but we weren't enemies. She usually kept to herself just like I did. I didn't have any friends but Prince. I saw the mean girls like Sierra and her crew always picking with Kimora, and I didn't understand why. The only thing they could say about her was that she was chubby because she had a very pretty face. In fact, she was gorgeous, and her hair was down her back.

I walked down the street, and cars honked at me, breaking my train of thought. I ignored each car that passed me because I wasn't that type of chick. I didn't talk to men who pulled up alongside me like I was a prostitute or something. That shit wasn't happening at all.

When I got on my block, I spotted Prince. I looked at him and smiled. I loved Prince. He was such a good person. Me and Prince had been friends since we were little. Our moms went to the same church, even though my momma was crazy as shit at times.

Prince was standing on the block with a couple of his friends. They didn't speak to me, and I didn't speak to them. I was glad that I was the girl who boys didn't notice. I never wanted that drama in my life. That's why I was so afraid to take Knox up on his offer. K was the type of dude who had all the girls falling over him, and I knew I didn't measure up.

As I neared Prince and his friends, Prince started to walk toward me.

"What's up, Spirit?" He smiled. He favored the singer August Alsina so much you would have thought that was his brother or something.

"Hey, Prince. What's going on?" I said as we began walking together.

Prince and his mother lived right next door to me.

"Shit much. Out here cooling it with the guys."

"I see, I see." I chuckled.

"Damn, you saw what happened today with my boy K?"

"I saw that. Man, that was messed up," I replied, shaking my head.

"Yeah, I know. I wish I would have made it out there in

enough time. I would've got him up out of that jam," he said, and I looked at him funny.

"Prince, no you wouldn't. You would've helped him fight, and then you would've been in jail right along with him."

"Yeah… you right." He laughed, and I smirked.

"But how you been, though? You aight?"

"I'm fine. Focusing on my studies so I can get as many scholarships as possible. "

"I know, right. With yo brainiac ass."

He chuckled, and I shoved him. Prince always teased me about being a smart ass. I couldn't help it, though. I was determined to make it out of the hood.

"How's yo' moms?" he asked me, and I grunted.

I couldn't tell the truth about what was going on behind closed doors, so I did what I always did when somebody asked about Sandra's ass.

"She's cool. You know how her and Henry do," I shrugged as I spoke on my father.

"Oh, aight. I only asked because moms said she ain't seen her in church, you know."

"Yeah, I know. Sometimes she doesn't wanna go. I guess it's because she's getting old," I replied as we came upon my front porch.

"Well, Imma get up with you later. Call me or something, and we can go get some food if you hungry later," he said, and I nodded.

Prince turned to walk off, but before he could, I stopped him in his tracks.

"Aye, Prince," I called out to him.

He turned around and faced me. "Yeah?"

"If you hear from Knox, tell him that I'm going to be praying about his situation and that I'm thinking about him." I blushed, and Prince smiled.

"Aight, bet! Let me find out you feeling that nigga K. You been giving that nigga the run around for the longest."

"Just do what I said, best friend," I said and laughed.

"I'm best friend now 'cause you want something from me. But, aight, man. I gotchu."

"Thank youuuu!" I sang out and went to open my front door.

Walking inside, I looked around at the couches being pushed out the window. And the nightstand pushed against the window. I wasn't even confused when I saw the mess that my mother had made. I knew what it stemmed from.

My momma walked into the living room with no shirt on, just her bra and some small shorts. Her hair was disheveled, and her eyes were wild. *Here we go again*, I thought.

"Ma!" I called out to her, but she was in her trance.

She didn't even acknowledge me. I hated when she was like this.

"Ma!" I called out to her again.

My mother continued to ignore me, and I walked over and grabbed her hand. She jumped at me with those wild eyes, and she smiled.

"Hey, baby, you're home," she said in a low tone.

"Yes, I'm home, Mama. Whatchu doing?' I asked as I led her to the couch.

"I'm lookin' for the angels that's supposed to come," she said and took a seat on the couch.

"Oh, okay. Where's Daddy?" I asked her, and she looked at me as if she didn't know what I was talking about.

"Never mind, Ma. Did you eat your candy?" I asked, speaking of her medicine.

She shook her head, and I sighed deeply. I knew she didn't because she was never like this when she took her medicine, and my stupid ass, worthless father wasn't gonna make sure she took it either.

I got off the couch and went in the kitchen to grab her medicine and a bottle of water out the fridge. I went back in the living room and handed her the bottle of water. She looked at me skeptically, but she grabbed the bottle of water and the pills. She took them, and I instructed her to open her mouth to show me that they were all gone.

"I hate that candy." She scoffed, and I laughed.

I loved my momma with all my heart. My mother was diagnosed with schizophrenia years ago. Ever since I was kid, all I could remember was her having these episodes. But when she was on her meds, she was perfectly fine. I mean, normal, as if she didn't try to jump off a bridge the night before. I used to be scared as shit of her when I was younger, but now I was used to it.

I heard keys jingling in the front door, and my focus at once went toward it. It was my daddy coming in the house. I didn't like dealing with him either. My daddy was a low key monster. One minute he was cool as a fan, and the next minute, he was as evil as they came. I hated when he was drunk. Those times were the worst.

I was an only child, and lord knows I've dealt with some shit. No one would know my story if I didn't tell them. That's why I went to school and did my thing because I was looking forward to going to college. I wouldn't be able to take it if I had to endure this shit for another year.

"My angel," my daddy's deep voice boomed.

"Hey, Daddy." I smiled sheepishly as he made his way over to me.

He bent down and kissed my cheek. I could smell the Miller High Life all over him, and I my face turned up in disgust. He walked over and kissed my mother on the cheek as well. She looked at him with loving eyes. I could see the love they held for each other, but they both were mentally fucked up, and I was a product of it.

"What's for dinner, baby girl?' he asked me, and I shrugged.

I wasn't his wife, my mother was. I was still technically a kid, and I had to take care of both my parents as if they were kids.

"I don't know. I didn't take anything out. As a matter of fact, I just got in not too long before you, Daddy."

"Oh, well I took out some porkchops this morning. You don't mind throwing them in the oven for me, do you?" he asked me, and I subtly rolled my eyes.

I actually did mind. I needed to study for this test that I had coming up, but he didn't understand that shit.

"No, I don't mind. I'll do it now," I said and headed into the kitchen. Tears clouded the rim of my eyes as I thought about never having a real childhood. I just needed a fucking break. I swear I couldn't do this shit anymore.

I prepared the porkchops, and then I put on a pot of rice and a can of mixed veggies. While that cooked, I headed upstairs to my bedroom to get more comfortable. I plopped down on my twin sized bed and took my books and study guide out of my backpack.

I tried to focus on the chemistry assignment, but my mind went to Knox. Damn, he was so fine to me. I played so hard to get with him, but I wanted him in the worst way. I mean, he and Prince were best friends, and when I was younger, I used to like Prince lot. But, we became friends. Eventually, the way I felt about him faded away.

Knox was the type of dude who made you weak in the knees with his chocolatey skin, chinky eyes, and low cut. I loved his smile. His teeth were so white he could've been an ad for Colgate. I felt so bad for him. Damn, and just when we were about to have a chance to get closer, this shit happens.

I lay across my bed daydreaming about him, wondering what it would've been like to go out with him. I opened my notebook to a blank sheet of paper and decided to write him a letter. I didn't know what I was going to write. Hell, I didn't know where I would send the letter to. I just wanted to write.

As I got lost in my trance of writing, I could smell the porkchops cooking and the rice. I hopped up from my bed and raced down the stairs. My arrival in the kitchen just in time because the rice was boiling over. I turned the rice off, and the veggies as well, and then I checked the porkchops. They looked as if they had about twenty more minutes in the oven. I decided to sit in the kitchen and wait for them to be done. I knew I didn't wanna go back up the stairs because I would've lost focus on the cooking.

My mother walked in the kitchen all smiles, and I knew then that her medicine had finally kicked in.

"Hey, beautiful." She smiled at me.

"Hey, Ma," I dryly replied.

This was a reoccurring theme with her. One minute she was bat shit crazy, and the next she was normal as hell. The next stage with this medicine is she's gonna be knocked out cold for the rest of the night. That's what it did to her. It made her feel better, and then it would put her down for hours.

"Mmmhmmm, it smells good in here. Whatchu cooking?" she asked me.

"Porkchops."

"Oh, that's your father's favorite. Well, okay, beautiful. I'm about to go lie down," she said and kissed me again before walking out the kitchen.

I just shook my head because this shit was sad.

After dinner was done, I fixed my dad's plate and walked it to the living room where he was sitting in his Lay-Z-boy chair with a brown liquid in his cup. I rolled my eyes upward and handed him his plate then went up to my bedroom.

WAKING UP OUT OF MY SLEEP BECAUSE I HAD FELT THE URGE TO pee, I jumped when I looked up and my father was standing above my bed. His dress shirt was open, and his belt was unbuckled. I was scared shitless in that moment. His eyes were glossy red, and I knew he was drunk as a skunk.

"Da… Daddy, what's wrong?" I asked him a low tone.

"Where's my fucking food?" he slurred, trying to hold himself up.

He was just that drunk that he looked like he was about to tip over. I was scared to answer him because I didn't know what he was gonna say or do.

"Daddy, I fixed your plate already," I said.

"You fucking black bitch. Stop lying. Get your ass up and fix my dinner," he growled as he grabbed me by my arm and pulled me out of bed.

"Daddy, stop it!" I screamed, trying to pry his hands from off my arms, but he wasn't hearing me.

I pulled so hard that I fell backward and landed on my butt on the floor of my bedroom.

"Your worthless bitch. You're worthless, just like that fucking mother of yours. Ain't worth two got damn cents," he ranted as he pointed at me with a stiff finger while tears fell from my eyes.

I hated when he got like this. He wasn't physically abusive, nor did he touch me in a sexual manner, but he was verbally abusive, and that was just as bad.

"Daddy, please go lie down. You're drunk," I pleaded with him.

"You want me to lie down 'cause you tryna be sneaky. Ain't nothing but a sneaky little hoe like ya momma. She was a hoe, and she taught you to be a hoe. I married a fucking hoe. A crazy hoe at that," he scoffed and then laughed.

I couldn't believe my ears. He was in rare form tonight.

"Daddy…" I pleaded.

I was sitting on my bedroom floor wishing like hell he would get out and just leave me alone. Because once this is all said and done, he won't remember any of this in the morning. I looked around my room and spotted my flip flops, so I stood up and raced to the corner then slid them on my feet. He was still talking crazy to me as he watched me run around the room.

I flew past him, out of my bedroom, and down the stairs. My mother was laid on the couch asleep in a comatose state because she was off that medicine. She didn't hear a thing. I shook my head as I looked at her.

I left out of the front door and started walking down the street. I lived in the hood and true enough this was Chicago but when you know people in your hood this shit was nothing to be walking around at 3 in the morning.

I couldn't stop the tears from falling as I thought about my parents and my life. As I approached the park on 55th street, I spotted a group of dudes. I didn't wanna walk past them, but I didn't wanna walk on the other side where a bunch of crackheads were gathered either. I didn't even know where I was walking to, but I needed to get out of that house before Henry's ass started really tripping.

"Aye, shawty, check it out," some dude called out to me, but I kept walking and ignored him.

"Fuck you then, bitch," he shouted, and the dudes laughed.

It irritated me so badly that I shocked myself when I said something back to him.

"Nigga, fuck you!" I screamed back.

That was not like me, but I had so much on my mind that I wasn't in the mood to be called out my name.

"Aye, Spirit?" I heard a familiar voice call out to me.

I stopped in my tracks and waited to see who it was. It sounded like Prince, but I wasn't too sure.

"Aye, hol' up!" Prince yelled, causing me to stop walking.

I wiped my tears with the back of my hand as I waited for Prince to jog over to me.

When he got up on me, his eyes were low, and I could tell he had been smoking weed or some shit.

"What's up? You good, sis?" he asked.

"No," I said and broke down crying.

He took me in his arms.

"What's up, man? Why you out here? Why you crying?" he asked as he hugged me tightly.

"I'm so... I'm so tired of this shit... I'm tired of it all," I sobbed as my emotions poured out of me.

"What happened, sis? Talk to me," he said in a soothing tone.

"My fucking parents are stressing me the fuck out! I can't take this shit," I sobbed.

I was sick and tired mentally and emotionally. Why couldn't my fucking life be normal for a while?

"C'mon, man, you don't need to be out here walking this fucking late by yourself," he said then grabbed my hand and walked me back the other way.

"I don't wanna go back home right now."

"You ain't got to. You can chill at my crib," he said, and I nodded.

We were silent the entire walk back to his crib, and my mind was running in circles. I didn't know what I was gonna do, but I knew I couldn't keep living like this. My momma and daddy were fucked up.

Once we got to Prince's crib, we headed to the basement where his room was located. I knew exactly where it was because I'd been down there numerous times. Entering the bedroom, I plopped down on Prince's bed, and he turned on the television.

"You want somethin' to eat?"

I giggled. "Nah, dude, it's three in the morning. I'm not hungry," I said, and he laughed with me.

"Yeah, you right. I'm hungry as shit, though," he said and walked out of the room to head for the kitchen.

He came back into the room minutes later toting a big ass sandwich and some Ruffles potato chips.

"Greedy butt," I sassed.

"Man, that weed be having a nigga hungry as fuck," he said as he smacked away at the sandwich.

"Where yo momma at?"

"She's sleep, muhfucka." He laughed.

"True."

"So, man, what's up? What's going on with yo' parents?" he asked me, and I swallowed hard.

I never told anyone about my parents. It was something that was hard to talk about, but I knew that I had to tell Prince. He wasn't gonna go for me just saying anything to him.

34

"My momma, she... she suffers from an illness."

"Oh damn, yo' momma sick? Why you ain't tell me that shit?"

"It's not like you think. She has a mental illness."

"Oh, damn, sis. I didn't know," he said, and I shrugged as my eyes watered.

"Oh, it's all good. Don't nobody know," I replied as tears fell from my eyes.

He took his thumb and wiped away my tears.

"Aye, man, it's gon' be aight. You gotta hold on, though, ma. Be strong 'cause she needs you."

"I know... I just get sooo... so... so tired." I wiped my tears with the back of my hand and laid my head on Prince's shoulder.

"Well, man, look. Anytime you need a fucking break, just hit me up. I'm always here for you, man, and you know that shit."

"I know," I whispered lightly and looked up in his eyes.

His eyes were so beautiful to me. They were big and hazel. Without thinking, I leaned in and kissed his lips. He pulled back and sort of frowned at me, which caused me to become embarrassed.

"I'm sorry."

"Don't be sorry. It's okay," he said.

When he said that, I leaned in and kissed him again. We started touching and pulling on each other, and then he pulled back again, which confused me.

"Aye, you sure, though?" he asked me with a raised eyebrow, and I nodded.

I don't know what came over me, but I wanted him to

touch me and hold me in the worst way. I wasn't a virgin because I had sex three times my freshmen year of high school with this dude I thought was gonna be my forever. But he showed me that he was a young nigga just like the rest. He took my virginity and played me after that. I was heartbroken, but I got over it.

Prince leaned in and gently kissed me. He started fingering my pussy, and after that, it was over. I gave Prince my body, and I didn't regret a moment of it until the next morning when we woke up. We were both asshole naked, and his mother was standing there looking at us.

"Spirit? Is this how you conduct yourself?" She grilled me, and I hung my head in shame as I scrambled for my clothing.

"I'm sorry, Mrs. Hughes."

"And it's Ms. I'm not married, and neither are you while you up in here fornicating with my son. I just bet you are sorry. Does your mother know that you're here?" she asked me, and I shook my head.

"Well, that's even more crazy. Go home, little girl, and Prince, hurry yo ass up and get out of here for school."

She grunted and walked out the room, slamming the door behind her. Once she was gone, Prince started busting up laughing. I mugged him.

"That shit is not funny, nigga!" I squealed as I put my shirt over my head.

"Man, Moms will be aight, but come here right quick." He motioned me with his finger, and I shook my head. But then I started to sashay back over to him.

Before I could get back to him, his mother came back into the room.

I jumped from the door opening, and she was still mugging me, but this time she was holding a phone in her hand.

"Spirit, what did I just tell you? It's time for you to go," she snapped.

I hurried and grabbed my shoes.

"The phone, boy, and get yo ass out that bed. You ain't paying no bills in here, Prince."

"Who is it, Ma?"

"It's Knox," she said and handed him the phone.

She walked out the door, still mugging me in the process.

Prince and I looked at each other before he got on the phone. I felt like a slut. I liked two best friends, and I just slept with one of them. Damn, I felt bad now. Knox wasn't my man, but damn, I liked him a whole fucking lot.

WHEN IT RAINS, IT FUCKING POURS

PRINCE

"**W**haddup, broski?" I said into the phone as I watched Spirit leave my bedroom.

She had a shamed look etched on her face, and I laughed to myself. This shit was crazy. I had never seen Spirit in that light before, but when my dick got hard, it thought with its own brain.

"What's good, bro? I'm just hitting you up. Shit, my bitch ass step momma ain't letting me talk to Kimora, so I need you to get at her for me."

"Okay, bro. So what they say?"

"Dude didn't make it, bro. I'm going down for murder," he said in a low tone, and I hung my head.

"Damn, bro," I whispered.

I couldn't believe my homie was about to be gone for a fucking murder.

"Yeah, man, I'm still in lock up, though. I'm using this nigga phone who knows my pops from the army. He's a cop, so he looked out for me. I can't be on this bitch long, bro."

"Aight, man. I gotchu. I'm gonna slide by y'all crib and holla at Mora." I told him

"Aight, thanks, bro. But how Spirit doing?" he asked me, and I swallowed hard.

The shit felt awkward as hell him asking me about her after I just smashed her the night before.

"She good, bro. Why you ask that?"

"Nah, I thought I heard ya moms say her name before you got on the phone."

"Yeah, she was here. You know we walk to school together sometimes."

"Oh yeah, that's right. Well, tell her I said what's up, bro," he said in a sad tone.

"I will, nigga. But you cool, though?"

"Hell yeah. I ain't worried, and you know that shit already," he said, and I laughed.

I knew K could hold his own. That nigga was just tough like that. He didn't give a fuck, and niggas learned the hard way when they got that shit twisted.

Me and K finished talking, and before he got off the phone, I promised him that I would go see Kimora and let her know what it was. After hanging up the phone with K, I finally got my ass out of bed and headed for the bathroom. I had to shower so I could take my ass to school. One thing my moms didn't play about was school, and I was trying my hardest to make her proud of me.

It's always just been me and my moms. She was all I had.

I had an older brother named Terror, but he rarely came around. He was in these streets getting money, and he refused to put me on. He refused to help our fucking momma, and the shit was sickening.

See, I was only eighteen, but Terror was in his thirties. My moms was old when she had me, but she still looked youthful. She acted youthful as well. She was a church going woman. A nigga ain't never had a pop in his life; it's always just been me and my moms.

She was an awesome woman who broke her back for me. And even though I hung in the streets with my niggas, I went to school.

As I stepped in the shower, I turned the water on, and my mind instantly went to Spirit. She was so fucking beautiful. I had never seen in her in a girlfriend type of light, but man, after how good her pussy was last night, I was thinking differently. Friends was all good, but now I was thinking we could be something more. She had always been my friend, and I've always cared about her wellbeing. I was shocked that she let me hit. Hell, I thought Spirit's quiet ass was a fucking virgin.

If I did wife her, I would hate to think what K would say, 'cause man, he really liked her ass. Knox was my fucking homie, so shit was awkward as hell to me.

Someone banging on the bathroom door startled me out of my thoughts.

"Yeah!" I shouted with a frown on my face.

"Boy, if you don't hurry yo ass up out of there, it's gonna be a problem, Princeton Maurice Bash!" my moms screamed my name, and I laughed.

"On my way out now, ma." I finished washing up and hopped out of the shower.

After dressing and looking at myself in the mirror, I headed out of the house. I walked down the street toward Mora and Knox's crib. When I got to the front door, I hesitated to knock because I hated their fucking step mother. After taking a deep breath, I knocked heavily on the front door, and it came open. That lil nigga, Trey, was standing there grinning and shit.

"What's up, Prince?' he announced excitedly.

"What's good, bro bro? Where Kimora?"

"She's in the kitchen."

"Can you go grab her for me real quick?" I asked his goofy ass.

"What the fuck you need with fat ass?" He laughed, and I frowned.

"Nigga, do it fucking matter? Just go and get her," I barked at him, and his face turned into a frown.

"Aight, man, be cool, damn." He huffed and walked away.

I never understood why muthafuckas picked on Mora. She was fucking drop dead gorgeous. That bitch, Sierra, was just a hater. I wasn't one to deny a fine ass shawty when I saw one.

Kimora came to the door moments later, and I saw the bandage that was on the side of her face. Her long hair was pushed back into a thick ponytail, her thick thighs were covered in some holey joggers, and she sported a t-shirt that looked as if it was supposed to be in the trash two years ago.

She didn't have to be a size six for me to think she was beautiful.

"Hey, Prince," she said in a low tone.

"What's up, Mora? Have you heard from K?"

"No." She shook her head.

"Well, he called me this morning. He's locked up, and they're gonna transport him to the county. They're charging him with murder," I told her, and tears welled up in her eyes,

"He… He killed him?" she said in a low tone as I just stared at her.

She was so fucking pretty. I didn't know why she had so little self-esteem. I mean, she was little on the chunky side, but still, that didn't mean shit. She was still gorgeous.

"Yeah, man, he said he's been trying to call, and he's not getting through, so I just wanted to let you know what he told me."

"Alright, thanks Prince," she said in a sad tone and turned and walked back in the house.

I stood there for a minute, not knowing what to say. Shit was going all wrong right now. Me and Spirit had sex, Knox was locked up. Shit just wasn't right.

I walked off the porch and headed to school. I guess it was time for me to get my day started. School was about to be over in three months, and that's all I was looking forward to. Walking across the state to make my momma proud.

Once school was over, I tried to catch up to Spirit, who

was walking as fast as she could to the bus stop. I called out to her, but she ignored me. She must've felt embarrassed about what we did earlier, but that didn't mean shit to me. She ain't have shit to feel ashamed of. I also looked around for Kimora. I wanted to make sure she was good.

I knew Knox wasn't anywhere around, and muthafuckas would try and pull it with her. That bitch, Sierra, was in school looking sad as fuck because her brother got killed, but she was the random bitch who started all that shit.

I made my way down the street. I was about to kick shit with the rest of my niggas and cool out since I didn't have shit to do. I should've been filling out job applications like my moms asked me to, but I didn't wanna do that shit.

I went up to Washington Park and met my mans, Hassan. He was sitting there with two bitches smoking weed. I dapped him and smiled at the shorties.

"What's good, bro? What's up, ladies?" I smiled at them.

"Heyyyy," they both said in unison.

"Hey, this my homie. Prince, this bad ass shorty right here, her name is Keisha," he said, introducing me to the short chick. She was thick as hell, and I couldn't help but lick my lips as I gazed down at her.

"What's up, Keisha?"

"Hey." She giggled.

"Yeah, bro. I got my uncle's whip' and we thinking about hitting the lakefront. You tryna slide with us?" he asked me.

Fuck it, I didn't have shit else to do today.

"Fuck it, c'mon," I replied and we all walked out of the park and headed for Hassan's whip.

As we were walking, I connected eyes with Spirit. She

looked at me, and I felt like shit. She held a smirk upon her face, and I shook my head. I didn't wanna leave shawty though. I was curious to see what she was about.

We hopped in Hassan's people's ride, and he drove us to the liquor store, and then we grabbed some more weed from one of the guys from around our hood. Afterward, we headed for the lake front where we sat and kicked it until night fall.

"Aye, bro, me and Shawnie will be right back," he said and grabbed shorty's hand that he was with. She was giggling and shit.

I watched Hassan smack her on the ass, and I already knew what they were about to do.

"So, what's up, shorty? You got a nigga or sum?" I asked her.

"No, I'm single. You got a girl?" she asked me, and I thought about Spirit.

"Nah, I'm single too." I grinne.

Fuck it, I was young, only eighteen years old, and I had my whole life ahead of me.

"Damn, yo ass fine," I whispered, looking into her eyes.

She smirked, and I took that as my cue to lean in and kiss her plump lips.

"Damn, them bitches juicy. Can I kiss you again?" I asked her, and she nodded.

I kissed her again, and this time, I put my hand on her thigh to see how far she would let me go.

We started going at it, and since we were in the cut and it was dark, I decided to see if she would let me fuck. And she did. I fucked her on the lake while my homie was smashing her friend in the whip. Once it was all said and done, we left the lake feeling like two of the luckiest niggas alive.

We pulled up to shorty's house that I was fucking with, and I walked her up to the door. She had a scared look on her face, and I couldn't help but notice it.

"You good, ma?"

"Yeah... yeah, I'm good. Do you know what time it is? My phone died a long time ago," she said.

"Yeah." I pulled out my phone and glanced at the clock.

"It's 1:45," I told her, and her eyes bucked.

"In the morning?" she damned near yelled.

"Yeah." I laughed.

"Oh my god, I gotta go. Tell yo homeboy thanks for the ride." She scurried off, and I shook my head.

I walked back to Hassan's car feeling like I was on cloud nine. Two days of pussy back to back, mannnn I was living the life.

Hassan dropped me off at the crib, and I went inside and crashed. I didn't take off my clothing or nothing. I lay across my bed and I was out.

"PRINCETON!! PRINCETON!!" I COULD HEAR MY MOM'S VOICE IN my sleep, and I hopped up out of instinct.

"Yeah, Ma?" I replied, agitated by her voice.

I squinted because there was a bright light shining in my face.

"What the hell are these police officers talking about,

46

boy?" she yelled, and that's when it registered. There were two detectives in my bedroom.

"I don't know. What y'all doing here?"

"They saying you raped a fourteen year old girl?"

"Raped? I ain't raped nobody, and especially no fourteen year old lil girl," I snapped at them.

"Son, it was semen found in the rape kit. We need you to get up and come down to the station with us. We have some questions for you," the detective said, and I got off the bed feeling nervous as hell.

I didn't know shit about what they were talking about.

They led me out of my crib in handcuffs while my mother cursed and fussed. But I was tryna wrap my brain around all the lil bitches I had fucked. I was eighteen, but I was sort of a playboy, and I fucked with a lot of chicks.

Once I got to the station, I was led into the interrogation room. That's when I found out that shorty I kicked it with tonight was only fourteen years old. Bitch had a body like she was seventeen, and she was mature as well. But I didn't rape the bitch. I didn't have to force a chick to do nothing they didn't wanna do.

I was held in lock up for seventy-two hours. They did a rush on the DNA sample, and it matched me. I knew it would. I knew I was up shit's creek. I didn't use a condom with her just like I didn't use one with Spirit. I was charged with rape of a minor and sent prison; disappointing myself and breaking my mother's heart in the process.

WHEN SHIT GETS WORSE

KIMORA

I was miserable as I sat in the house looking out the window of my bedroom. I didn't care what anyone said to me, I wasn't ever going back outside. Three months had passed since my protector, my big brother, the only person who ever had my back was gone. I hadn't left the house since that day. I didn't attend my high school graduation, prom, nor luncheon. I didn't wanna be seen in public anymore.

Candice thought I was going crazy because I didn't wanna go out. She told my dad, and even though he was away, he ordered for a therapist to come and talk to me, but it was like she was talking to herself because I wouldn't say shit to her. Sierra had permanently scarred me. The therapist told Candice and my dad that I was suffering from a disorder called agoraphobia.

I still remember the day she said I had whatever that shit is. I could hear her talking, but I only ignored everyone around me.

"So, Dr. Taylor, what do you think is wrong with her? She hasn't said a word to anyone since her incident at school," Candice said like she was loving mother or something, but she was far from it.

I stared out the window and ignored them.

"Well, Mrs. Eldredge, when someone experiences a traumatic event, they may have a hard time accepting some things."

"And not talking and going out the house is it? Because it's weird if you ask me," Candice added.

I rolled my eyes even though she couldn't see me.

"It's weird to you, but to the people going through it, it's not weird at all. See, agoraphobia is a profoundly difficult anxiety disorder. It's also a disorder that's difficult to explain and is often caused by other anxiety disorders in many different ways. Agoraphobia is often misunderstood as its definition can change depending on how some things have an effect on them. Some have the fear of being out in the environment around them."

"I still don't get it, but okay. So, what can we do to get her out of this funk she's in? Her father will be here really soon, and I don't want her acting like this." She scoffed, but that was news to me.

I didn't even know my father was on his way home already.

"It's all up to her. Right now, she's going through something traumatic. Agoraphobia affects people in many ways. Her disorder may affect her ability to leave the house. This is her protective zone, and she fears being in harm's way if she leaves this home. People who suffer from agoraphobia also fear being out in the open or a public place, fear of being in an area with no easy *escape, fear of being in unfamiliar places, or fear of leaving their home."*

"Now that's some deep shit right there. I've never heard of that."

"Many illnesses receive little attention because they are uncommon," the doctor said. "She's very young, so she should get past this. I would recommend that you give her time and let her grieve whatever loss she's suffering from," the doctor suggested.

I tuned her out as Candice started talking about other shit.

Coming to from my flashback, I thought about how Sierra attacked me When I came out of school that day, she was standing there with her brother and his friends, and also her friends. She pulled out a razor blade and sliced me down my face. I had to get twenty-four stitches in my face. I felt like the fucking ugly duckling. After I learned that Knox was in jail because he murdered Sierra's brother with that brick, my universe fell apart.

Knox was facing twenty years in prison. My dad had gotten him a lawyer, and he was still going back and forth to court. They were going to take it to trial. Sitting at home, I couldn't help but wonder why I couldn't have my own mother. I needed somebody to talk to. Somebody to help me when shit gets rough. Man, I missed my momma so fucking much.

A knock on my bedroom door startled me, and I jumped from the sound. The door came open, and in walked Candance with a frown on her face. She was holding a bucket of water, and I was confused on what she was doing with it.

"You think your fat ass is gonna sit in this room all

fucking day and not do shit? Huh? Snap out of that shit, you crazy bitch!" Candice yelled at me.

I looked back at her and didn't respond. I continued to stare out the window, completely ignoring her. My world was falling apart, and I just didn't know what to do. I hadn't heard my father's voice yet, and he was supposed to have been home. Even when he asked to speak to me, I refused to talk to him. I just couldn't think of anything to say.

"Bitch, you don't hear me talking to you?" Candice shouted, and still, I ignored her.

Then, unexpectedly, I felt ice cold water hit my skin, and I yelped out in pain as the water felt like small needles hitting my backside.

"Whyyyy, would you do that?" I screamed, hopping up and running up in her face.

I was so fucking angry. I didn't do shit to this bitch, and she fucked with me every chance she got. Her and her fucking son.

"Oh, you think tough, you fat bitch? If you don't get the fuck out of my face." She scowled, and I mugged her.

I was sick and fucking tried of Candice's ass. When I didn't move, she took the pot she was holding and hit me with it. I fell to the floor, where she preceded to beat me with the fucking pot like I was nothing. Fighting back was to no avail because physically, she was stronger than me. I hadn't been eating, and I knew I was weak, so I just stopped trying because it wasn't worth it.

Once Candice got tired, she walked out of my bedroom, and I threw myself on my bed and cried my eyes out. This couldn't be life right now for me. It just couldn't.

Lying in bed, it seemed like time just ticked by. I didn't leave the house for nothing in the world. There was no urge to even wash my ass. I was suffering from depression, and I knew it. A week had passed since that incident with Candice, and if I stayed out of her way, I knew I would be okay. Knox had been calling, but I didn't wanna talk to him. I felt like it was my fault he was in the predicament that he was in now

I looked at the clock that sat on my nightstand, and it was midnight. Sleep wouldn't come easy for me at all. I got out of bed and headed to the bathroom. I finally ran a hot shower and climbed in it. The water hitting my skin felt so good. It felt like I hadn't bathed in months.

Once I was done, I climbed out of the shower, stood in front of the bathroom mirror, and stared at my reflection. My scar was healing nicely, but I still felt like I was the ugly duckling. I left out the bathroom and went to my bedroom and lay across my bed staring at the ceiling.

I couldn't believe what I was going through, and I couldn't wait for the day when I had as much confidence as the next girl. In the fall, I would be nineteen years old, and I had never even kissed a boy. Never been complimented by men before in my life. My life wasn't shit but a dead end.

I closed my eyes and eventually drifted off to sleep, but then I was awakened suddenly when I felt somebody on top of me. My eyes popped open, and Trey's ass was on top of me.

"What are you doing?" I yelped, and he clamped his hand down over my mouth.

He pulled up my nightgown and forcefully pried my legs

apart. I tried to scream as it registered in my brain what the fuck he was doing to me. He was about to rape me.

Please, God, don't let him do this to me, I thought

"Shut the fuck up, fat ass!" he growled as he used his free hand to pull his small penis out.

My thighs were extra thick, so he was having a hard time trying to fight me off and position himself so that he could get in me. I looked toward my bedroom door because I saw a shadow move in the darkness, and tears fell from my eyes as I watched my little brother stand in the doorway watching me get violated by Trey.

When Trey couldn't take it anymore, he swung and punched me in the face.

"Bitch, I said stop fucking moving!" he growled, and I stopped.

The blow to my face hurt so bad that I didn't even wanna fight anymore. He finally was able to position himself in front of me, so he could get in good. When he did, I cringed in pain as he broke my hymen. He started to hump on me like a dog in heat, and I cried the entire time. I clamped my eyes shut because I just wanted the shit to be over with.

After about five minutes, I heard a deep voice say, "What the fuck is going on here?"

With that, I opened my eyes, and my daddy was standing there. He grabbed Trey off me and tossed him into my bedroom dresser.

"Get the fuck off my daughter, you son of a bitch!" Daddy screamed.

I sat up in my bed sobbing as I pulled the covers over me, and my daddy commenced to beating his ass.

"Wait, what's going on?" Candice tried to say until she noticed my father in the room beating Trey's ass.

"Louis! Louis! Please! You're hurting him!" she cried as she watched her only son get almost beat to a pulp.

My father was an older man, but he was a military man.

"Get him the fuck out of my house, Candice, and now!

"Louis, don't do this. He has nowhere to go," she begged, but he still wouldn't listen. He beat Trey's ass until he was bloody.

"I don't give a fuck! No got damn rapist is gonna be living in my house! He just tried to rape my daughter!" Daddy yelled.

"Louis, please! He didn't mean it!" Candice cried.

"Get him the fuck out of my house! Now!" he shouted at her, and she picked a bleeding Trey up and helped him walk out of my bedroom.

I was half naked, scared, and crying.

"Baby girl," my daddy's deep baritone voice boomed through the room.

"Hi, Daddy," I said in a low tone and began to sob.

I had missed him so much. He leaned in to hug me, and when he did, I hugged him so tight and didn't wanna let him go. He kissed the top of my forehead.

"Shhhh, shhhh, it's gonna be okay, beautiful. Daddy's home. I promise I'm never leaving again," he said.

It was a comfort to know my father was back. To hear him say he was never leaving me again, I felt so good about that.

After crying and hugging my daddy, he got up and left my bedroom, and that's when I noticed the limp that he had.

I didn't know what happened to his leg, and I wasn't in the mood to ask questions.

I got out of my bed and went in the bathroom to clean the scent of Trey off my body. I was becoming more and more broken as the days ticked by, and I didn't know what I ever did in my life to make people treat me the way they did. But little did I know, my life would only get worse.

THIS SOME BULLSHIT

KNOX

"I nmate KO1455, visitor!" the CO yelled, coming up on my cell.

I put down the book I was reading and got out of my bunk. I'd been locked up now for three months. My father's lawyer was able to get me off on the murder charge, and they only charged me with manslaughter. I took a plea deal and was sentenced to eight years in prison. Because I was eighteen years old, juvie was out of the question.

I walked through the gates and was led to the visitation area. My pops was sitting there, and a smile overcame me. Damn, I missed him.

"What's up, Pops?"

I smiled as I walked up on him, and he hugged me tight. We both took our seats, and pops stared at me for a minute before he said anything.

"You know, son, I don't even have the words to say that I want to say. I'm not angry at you, but I'm not proud either. I understand—"

"Pops," I tried to say, but he held his hand up to cut me off.

"Nawl, just listen, son. As I was saying, I understand why you did what you did when it came to Kimora, but what I'm not understanding is that rage that you have built in you. Candice told me how you went around cursing her out and being disrespectful, and I didn't raise you like that, boy," he said.

My pops had me fucked up. He was taking the word of that evil ass bitch and not even giving me a chance to explain anything.

"She told you all of that, huh?"

"Yeah, son, she did."

"Did she tell you how she calls Kimora out her name when she thought I wasn't looking? Or that she starves her when she wants to? Did she tell you she lets Kade and Trey get high in the garage because they want to? Nah, she can only tell you some shit I said, and you gonna believe her 'cause you fucking her!"

"Boy, watch ya gotdamn mouth. I don't give a damn how old ya are! I'm your father!" he barked, and it seemed like the visiting room got quiet and everyone was staring at us.

I sucked my teeth and folded my arms across my chest.

"If all of this was going on, why didn't you or Kimora say anything? If Candice was so bad, why am I just now hearing about it? Now, her son, Trey, his worthless as got put out of my house. I'm no father of his."

"Pops, let be real. How often are you home? How long do you actually stay when you are home? You placed Candice in our life as a replacement for Moms, and she'll never be Moms. And Trey, that lil nigga was a piece of work. So, you put Candice and him out?" I asked, curious to know, and he shook his head.

"Nah, just his ass. I caught him trying to rape Kimora when I first came home. No one knew I was coming home. I tried to surprise them, and when I went into Kimora's bedroom to wake her up, I found that piece of shit on top of my daughter, stealing her innocence," he growled and stared off.

I could tell it was still fucking with him. My nostrils flared, and I got irritated all over again. That bitch ass nigga, Trey. He was lucky I'm locked up because I would've killed him with my bare fucking hands.

"Man, this some bullshit," I hissed, fuming mad.

This lil nigga thought shit was sweet, and I hated that I was in this jam right now.

"So, the bitch Candice ain't gone?" I asked him.

I was confused. How in the fuck did she let my pops put her son out but not her?

"No."

"And why the FUCK not?" I yelled at him.

"Knox, she's my wife, and she didn't do anything wrong. I'm not gonna put her out. If she wanted to leave, she could have, but she didn't. She allowed his father to come and get the worthless piece of shit off of my porch."

I let out a deep sigh and shook my head. My old man be

fucking up. I didn't know what it was about this broad, Candice, but she's had his nose wide open.

"What happened to yo leg, Pops?" I asked him, deciding to drop the subject. I wasn't gonna do nothing but make myself angrier about the situation that I had no control over.

"It's nothing, son. Nothing a little pain pills can't cure. It comes with the job," he responded, and I only nodded.

Me and my pops continued to chat it up until visiting hours were over. Once he got up to leave, he hugged me tight, and it felt like that was the last time that I was gonna see him. Walking back to my cell, I passed the line of newcomers, and my eyes bucked when I spotted my nigga Prince. He didn't look scared; he only looked confused. I nodded my head at him when we made eye contact.

It had been three months since I heard from him. The last time I talked to Prince, I asked him to go to my house to holla at Kimora for me, and that was it. I tried calling his house phone, but I never received an answer. I chopped it up as his moms didn't want nobody to be calling her phone collect.

I couldn't shake the thought of Prince off my mind as I entered my cell. I sat on my bunk and wondered what the fuck did this nigga do to be in a maximum security prison. This shit wasn't cool at all. Me and my homie couldn't be in this jam like this.

ME AND PRINCE WEREN'T ON THE SAME CELL BLOCK, SO I OFTEN wondered where he was. I wanted to make sure he was cool.

I knew my nigga could hold his own, but he still wasn't built like me.

Lunch time came around, and we all entered the cafeteria. My eyes scanned the crowd to see if I spotted Prince, and I did. He was sitting at a table with some niggas who must have been newbies as well. I mean, I've only been there for three months, but that didn't mean shit. I was a young bull, and when these niggas tried it with a nigga, it was nothing for me to defend myself. I would fight to the death if it meant demanding my respect.

After grabbing my tray with my food, I walked over to where Prince was seated and plopped down next to him. He looked at me, and a smile erupted on his face.

"What's good, broski?" I smiled as we dapped each other up.

"Shit, nigga," he scoffed, but I was waiting for him to tell me what was.

How the fuck did he end up in this joint?

"How the fuck you get up in here?" I questioned him.

He looked around before he answered me.

"Nigga, a long story."

"Okay, nigga, I'm waiting. It don't look like I'm going nowhere no time soon." I chuckled.

"Man, some shawty said I raped her," he replied, and my eyes bucked.

"Get the fuck out of here, man, you lying."

"I wish I was fucking lying, but the crazy thing is I didn't use a rubber when I smashed her, and my semen was found in her. So, yeah, it looks like I'm lying and she's telling the truth." He shrugged but I can tell it fucked with him.

It would've fucked with me too if I was falsely accused of some bullshit.

"Mannnn, that's fucked up."

"Tell me about it."

"You been good though?" I asked, taking a bite of the bread.

"I'm good, nigga. Just wanna do my time and stay in my lane."

"Yeah, I know right?" I replied.

Me and Prince chopped it up until it was time to go out to the yard. This was the only time I would be able to fuck with my mans because they had us separated.

Once I was back in my cell, I pulled out a pen and some paper and decided to write my sister a letter. I missed Kimora so fucking much, and I hoped like hell she was okay. What that bitch ass nigga, Trey, tried to do to her wouldn't go unanswered, I can guarantee that shit. I didn't care how long I'm locked down for, I was gonna make sure I got that bitch ass nigga

As I wrote my letter lost in my own thoughts, one of the newbies ran to my cell in a hurry.

"Aye, bro, they got yo mans hemmed up in the shower," he stated, breathing hard as fuck with a scared look on his face.

I dropped the paper, but I still held on to the pen as I raced out of my cell toward the showers. Once I got there, niggas were huddled all around. This big ass nigga named Frost had told his minions to hem Prince up in the shower, and we all knew Frost was a booty boy. He liked to break mufuckas in, but he had my homie fucked up.

Prince was fighting for dear life, but it was too many of them. I instantly ran over there and swung my fist, knocking the shit out of the one dude who held onto Prince' arms. He let them go and tried to bum rush me. We fell in the shower, and I started beating dude's ass.

That newbie who came to tell me what was going on attacked the other nigga who was holding Prince. Once he did that, Prince was free, and he headed straight to Frost's bitch ass. Prince was a pretty boy ass nigga, but he was a beast with this shit. He could beat some ass as well.

We fucked them big old ass niggas up until the guards raced in. They took too long, which let me know that Frost had already put them on game. What they didn't know was that Frost and his niggas were going to the infirmary instead of Prince.

Once we were handcuffed and led down to segregation (the hole), the guards tossed me onto the concrete floor, and I laughed to myself. Fuck them! I was gonna make these bitch ass niggas respect the name Knox!

"Aye, bro, good looking out," Prince yelled.

"My brother for life!" I yelled back.

"Aye, newbie, what's yo name?" I hollered out at the dude who helped us.

"Benz," he shouted back.

"Good shit, Benz!" I yelled, recognizing how he came through for us in that moment.

After talking shit across the way, the guards instructed us to be quiet. I did, but I couldn't sleep, even though the room was dark as fuck. I was gonna be the most respected mutha-fucka in this joint. I wasn't backing down to none of these niggas and would lay hands each and every fucking time they tried me and my homies.

Fuck that, I was plotting a takeover, and respect was gonna be in high fucking demand. These niggas had the right nigga. They thought they were gonna make an example out of me and mine.

Love, Loyalty,& Revenge.

THROUGH THE FIRE

6 YEARS LATER, 2018

KIMORA

Looking myself over in the mirror, it amazed me that I had gained so much weight. I was wayyyy bigger than what I used to be when I was still in high school. I knew what it was, though. It was depression. My life had fallen apart. I mean, it was worse now than it was in the beginning.

My father, the vibrant man who was full of life, was nothing more than a shell of what he used to be. Everything my dad represented was now gone because he was addicted to heroin.

When my daddy came home that night he caught Trey in my bedroom, it was because he had gotten honorably discharged from the army. Something happened to him that he never talked about. I didn't pressure him because he never pressured me, but he was taking pain killers for the pain in his legs.

Then, the bitch, Candice, got my daddy hooked on drugs. We didn't have anything in our once beautiful home anymore. Anything they bought was now gone; we didn't have furniture, appliances, a television or none of the stuff we used to have. I now slept on the floor in my bedroom because I didn't have a bed anymore. I was miserable, and every day I thought about ending my existence. I hated Candice so much. I hated the ground she walked on. She took my father under, and he allowed her to.

The last time I took a step out the front door was six years ago. I haven't left the house since what happened to me in high school. When I was hungry, I would steal my daddy's credit card before he could spend the money off of it and use it to go grocery shop on this app called Instacart. My daddy still had his cell phone because he needed it to contact the veteran agencies and all of that. That's really the only thing of value he held on to besides his debit card with his benefits on it. Besides that, we had nothing.

Tears rolled down my face as I read the letter from Knox. I missed my brother so much. My better half, my twin. He was my strength when I was weak, and over these years, I had become weak. I was twenty-four years old and not doing anything with my life. I was too scared to face the outside world.

My little brother, Kade, who was now twenty-three years old, had moved out and hadn't been back since. He didn't even recognize me as his oldest sister, and he didn't show me an ounce of love. He didn't respect me, and he blamed me that Trey got put out. It just made me sick to my stomach that he would act like that toward me.

A knock on my bedroom door caused me to look up.

"It's open," I said.

The door opened, and my daddy came inside.

"Beautiful, good morning," he said, coming into my room scratching his skin.

I frowned a little bit but then replaced it with a smile. No matter what, he was still my daddy, and I loved him so much. Flaws and all.

"Hey, Daddy."

"Are you okay, princess?" he asked me.

"I'm okay. Are you okay, Daddy?" I asked him.

"No, I'm not, princess, but I promise you I'm gonna get better. I'm going to rehab, and when I do, I'm coming back better than I ever been before." He smiled, and I only nodded.

He'd said this to me time and time again, but it never happened. He always said some off the wall shit but was right back getting high with Candice.

"Where's your wife?" I asked him.

"She's not here." He shrugged.

"Daddy, she hasn't been here for the last two days," I expressed, and his wild eyes just looked at me.

"I know, Princess, and I know you don't like her. Hell, I don't like her anymore, now. But when the time comes, she's gonna get left," he said, and I didn't respond.

He always said shit like that, but he didn't do anything about it.

Boom, boom, boom!

I jumped from the sound. It sounded like the police were beating on the front door. I looked at my daddy, and he had a scared look on his face.

"Who is that, Daddy?" I asked in a low tone.

"Hide in your closet, princess," he said, and I was confused.

Hide? I wasn't some small chick. I couldn't just hide anywhere.

"What?"

"Kimora, stop talking crazy and do as I say! Now!" he slightly shouted, and I did as he said.

I was scared as shit as I hid in the closet. My body trembled with fear.

I could hear my daddy's footsteps as he walked toward the front door, and when he got there, I heard voices. The voices traveled to the bedroom, and when he walked past my room, I could hear the men talking in an aggressive tone to him.

"Where's my fucking money?" the man said, and I was confused.

"Aye, man, my wife said she paid you." My dad's voice trembled.

"Your wife ain't paid me shit. You the fucking junkie who owes me. Now where in the fuck is my money?" the man growled, and his voice was something I would never forget.

"I... I... I don't have it."

"You don't have it? Nigga, the fuck you mean you don't have it? Do I look like the type of nigga that play about my fucking money? You fucking junkie," the man shouted

"Pl... Please... sa—"

"Nigga, don't fucking beg. It's not a good look on you, Captain," the man said, taunting my father, and then he laughed.

"End this bitch ass nigga's existence," the dude said.

A gun went off, and I had to clamp my hand over my mouth as tears fell from my eyes. He killed my daddy, he just killed my daddy, was the only thing I thought as grief overtook me.

I heard footsteps walk past, and I held my breath until I heard the front door close. Then and only then did I come from my hiding place.

I walked out of my bedroom and scanned the living room, but I didn't see my dad. I dreaded walking to the back of the house where his room was located. When I did, what I saw caused my knees to buckle. My daddy, one of my best friends, my protector, was lying there, eyes wide open and lifeless.

"NOOOOOOOOOOOOOO," I released a gut-wrenching scream from the pits of my soul.

I couldn't believe this was happening to me. I couldn't believe my daddy was gone. I cried my heart out. I couldn't even get up and call 911.

This was the third worst day of my life. First my momma, second was Knox, and now my daddy was gone forever.

I SAT SLUMPED ON THE LIVING ROOM FLOOR OF MY HOUSE. Candice finally came home two days ago, and I was stuck in a trance with nothing to say to her. She was pathetic. Everything my father did for her, and she wasn't there when those niggas took his life. I had to will myself to call the ambulance to come.

My father's funeral was in three days, and that was a day that I was not ready for. I hadn't stepped foot outside the house in six years, and I didn't know how I was gonna do it. I didn't know if I could do it, but for my daddy, I would.

We were waiting for my daddy's lawyer to show up, and Candice could barely control herself. She paced the carpet and I thought she was gonna burn a hole in it. I couldn't stand her ass. She scratched her arms and talked to herself as I stared at her.

Candice looked down at me and stopped in her tracks.

"What the fuck are you looking at?" she growled.

I didn't respond because Candice was just ignorant like that. She wanted to start some shit with me for nothing, and now since my father was gone, this gave her the perfect opportunity to do so.

"Bitch, yo fat ass don't hear me talking to you?" she growled, and I still just stared at her.

"You don't hear me? You overgrown, lazy ass, whale. The minute that lawyer gets here, I'm putting yo miserable, fat ass out on the streets. You won't have no other choice but to leave this muthafucka," she spewed, and I still didn't respond, only pissing her off further.

"Bitch, you don't hear me, huh? Ya daddy ain't here to protect yo ass nah, is he?" she smirked, and that made me frown.

She had made a mockery out of my father's death. Like that was cool.

"I heard you, but I don't care," I replied, and a look of shock washed over her face.

"What the fuck did you just say to me?" She walked over and bent down in my face.

"You heard me. I DON'T CARE!" I shouted in her face, and she hauled off and smacked the shit out of me without warning.

In that instant, I stood up. Mean mugging her ass, I smacked the shit out of her back. She wasn't expecting that, and I could tell.

"Ohhhhh, bitch, you wanna fight, huh?" She started to circle me like she was Mike Tyson.

It was quite comical at this point because Candice was now frail and thin as hell. She didn't have it in her to fight anymore. This time, I was ready. I was gonna take out all of my pain and frustrations on her ass.

Before we could do anything else, a knock on the front door stopped us. Candice mugged me as she walked to the front door. When she swung the door open, standing there was the most beautiful older woman. she was dressed in a pants suit, and her sandy brown hair was cut short in a bob length style.

"How in the fuck can I help you?" Candice scowled as she stared at the beautiful woman.

"I'm here for Candice Eldredge and Kimora Eldredge," she announced with a bright smile.

"I'm Candice," she said, and I had to laugh to myself. This lady was a whole trip.

73

"And I'm Kimora," I said, finally speaking up.

"Good morning, ladies. I'm Jessica Ware. I was Mr. Louis Eldredge's attorney. I have some of his personal affairs that we need to get in order," she said, and Candice allowed her to continue talking.

"Affairs like what? How much did the nigga leave me?" Candice spewed, and I couldn't believe my ears.

The lady looked at her with shock written on her face.

"Okay, sooo..." she started.

She couldn't sit anywhere because we didn't have any furniture in the living room. She was standing up and fumbling with her suitcase. Finally, she got the papers out of her briefcase then looked over at us and started to read.

"Okay, so as far as the reading of the will goes, it starts off with Kimora Eldredge. My dearest, Princess. Life hasn't been easy for you, and this I understand. Being a military man, I really couldn't show my emotions like you needed me to. I wish I was there for you better than what I have shown. I'm sorry that I wasn't the father you would have wanted me to be, but I love you and your brothers with everything in me, and I'm sorry. I leave to you everything. You were my beneficiary, I also list Kade and Knox to receive a certain amount from the in heritance as well. I love you, princess, and always remember you are special and you're worth something. Love always, Daddy."

After the lawyer finished reading my father's message, the tears that fell from my eyes wouldn't stop flowing. I needed to hear that message.

"And then, to my dear wife, Candice Eldredge. You have given me nothing but grief. I allowed you to take me down as a man. You hurt me to the core by getting me hooked on drugs. You knew I was weak, and instead of lifting me up, you held me down. I've watched you in secrecy mistreat my only daughter. And for that, I leave you nothing but the four walls surrounding you. The house that you loved so much is all that I leave you with. I loved you, Candice, more than I should have, and for that, I am at fault," she said, and that was it.

I couldn't believe my ears. He didn't leave the bitch a damn dollar, and for that, I was happy as fuck! I smiled so hard that I thought my face would crack.

"Hol' the fuck up? So whatchu saying is that old, greasy muthafucka didn't leave me shit but this raggedy ass house?" Candice screamed.

The lady, Jessica, stared at her. I burst into laughter, and I just couldn't stop laughing. Candice looked over at me, and I laughed ever harder.

"No ma'am, I'm sorry. He came in about a month ago looking really bad. I have never seen Louis like that, but he wanted to change his will and move some things around. I didn't know of the letters until after his death when I was instructed to read them," the lady explained, and Candice had a look of sheer disappointment etched on her face.

"You gotta be fucking lying. That muthafucka wouldn't do this to me! He wouldn't do this to me!" she screamed.

I was still giggling when she walked over and got in my face.

"You think this shit is funny? Since you laugh so fucking much, get cho shit and get the fuck out! Get the fuck out!" she screamed, and out of the blue, she grabbed my long hair before I could do anything to stop her and started dragging me to the front door.

I clawed and screamed at her to let me go, but she wasn't hearing it. She was in rare form.

"Miss! Miss! Please…. Calm down, ma'am," Jessica said, but Candice wasn't hearing her.

She continued to pull me to the door. Once I was there, she let my hair go, and I kicked at her with all might. I caught her in the stomach, and she doubled over in pain. I hopped off the floor and went straight for her, swinging wildly and not caring where my punches connected or even if they connected at all. All I knew was that I wanted to inflict as much pain on her like she did to me.

I knocked the shit out of Candice, and she fell backward. Before I could hit her again, Jessica came over and grabbed me.

"Please, Kimora, just calm down," she whispered, holding me back.

Tears fell from my eyes because I was mentally and physically tired of her ass. I couldn't stand this bitch, and I made a vow that I would get her back for all the pain she caused me if it was the last thing I did.

"Get the fuck out of my house, you fat bitch! Get the fuck out before I call the police!" she screamed at me.

"Fuck you, bitch! I hope you fucking overdose!" I spat at her as Jessica led me out the door.

This time, I wasn't nervous to leave the house. This time, I felt free. I knew it was time.

THREE WEEKS HAD PASSED SINCE THE INCIDENT WITH CANDICE. My father's funeral passed, and it was a sad service. My father was a man of dignity and pride, and he succumbed to being nothing. Someone took his life away, and he was gone forever.

"Hey, are you hungry?" a voice startled me.

Jessica was standing in the doorway holding a sandwich and a bag of potato chips. I smiled at her and shook my head. She came in the bedroom and plopped down on the bed next to me. I didn't look at her because her beauty scared me, and I didn't wanna feel intimidated by her looks. Jessica's beauty was astounding.

She grabbed me underneath my chin and turned my head to look at her.

"Hey, are you okay?" she asked.

I shook my head. I wasn't okay.

"Let me tell you something, Kimora. You are very beautiful, don't ever feel like you're not. You are worthy of so much in life, and all you need to do is have confidence in yourself. Never let anyone make you feel as if you were less than," she spoke, and tears fell from my eyes.

I did feel like I wasn't worthy. I never heard I was beautiful by anyone except for Knox, but he wasn't here anymore.

"Thanks," I managed to say.

"You don't have to thank me. You don't have to do anything for me but become stronger. Never let anyone see you at the lowest point of your life. Do you understand me? You have what it takes to be something great. You ain't just a fat slob, you aren't a bitch, you're nothing but a beautiful, intelligent, queen. It's time for you to rise up and know your worth. Your father isn't here anymore, and neither is Knox. You can't let someone who only has negative energy in them ruin you."

"Why are you helping me, Jessica?" I asked.

I wanted to know her motive because I'd been staying with her since Candice put me out of her house. She took me right in. I wasn't a bother, though. I tried to stay out the way. I barely ate anything. Hell, I barely came out of the bedroom she had me in.

"Your father was a very good friend of mine. As matter of fact, if I'm honest, and I don't want you to hate me because of it or your father, but me and your dad used to have a relationship a long time ago. I first met Louis while in college. He used to go for computer programming, but he stopped going when he enlisted in the service. We broke it off when we decided to go into opposite directions. I fell in love with someone else, and he met your mother. Through it all, we were still friends.

Once your mother was battling cancer, he became depressed, and he needed a shoulder to lean on. I was going through a nasty divorce, so we were each other's comfort at that time in our lives. It was never meant to become a sexual relationship, but in life, some things happened. We broke it off immediately because the guilt both of us had on our hearts, we couldn't take it.

"I always regretted having an affair with your dad. We were the best of friends, and if he needed me, he should have come to me. That's why I was so disappointed in him when he came to see me, and he was down on his luck. That wasn't the man I knew. I've never seen Louis so broken, and I knew that it had everything to do with that damn wife of his.

"But when he came and saw me, he told me that he had a drug problem, but he didn't forget about you and your brothers. No matter what he did, he did not take any of the money he had from his inheritance."

"Inheritance? What did my father inherit?" I asked.

"Oh, you didn't know?" she asked with a raised eyebrow.

"No."

"Well, to be frank, your father didn't have to work a day in his life because he inherited money from his father who was in the oil business. He made millions over the years, which in turn was left to your father, but your grandfather didn't give him the easy way out. Your father had to earn his money like a man, and that's when he first enlisted in the military. He never once used that money to finance anything. He barely touched it. Candice didn't even know he had it, and when the time was right, he turned it all over to you. Kade and Knox have money too, but you have all of it. In other words, Kimora, you are filthy fucking rich," she said.

I broke out into the widest grin I could muster up. My heart started pounding, and my hands got sweaty. This shit didn't seem real.

"You have to go the bank and sign some papers. You already have an account set up, but your father's name is on it. We have to take the death certificate up there, and after the whole set up, you will have your own money, in your own account. How does that sound?"

She smiled, and for a moment, I was speechless. It was so much that I didn't know about my father.

"It sounds like a dream come true," I said in a low tone.

I didn't really know how to react. I guess I had to see it to believe it. I wouldn't know how real it was until I actually saw some money in my account. Even though the money made me happy, I would trade that in a heartbeat to have my daddy back. All I could think about was him. But I can say he's finally back with my momma where he belonged.

"It is a dream come true, Kimora. I don't know if you will trust me, but I want you to. Your father was a good man, and an awesome friend to me. When I was down and out, he always had my back, and I will forever love him. You are a part of him, and I will have your back as well. I wanna show you how it's okay to live, sweetheart. You've hidden from the world for too long, and it's time to come back. You deserve everything that God has in store for you. Don't ever think otherwise," she said, and I nodded.

"Thank you, Jessica."

"No thanks needed, Mora. I'm going to take a shower and freshen up. We can go shopping afterward. Are you feeling up to it?"

"Yeah." I smiled, and she patted my shoulder as she left out the room.

I knew I had a long road ahead of me, but with my newfound wealth, I was sure I was gonna make the best out of my life. I felt like a burden had been lifted off my shoulders, or better yet, the devil had removed himself from my life, and God gave me an angel by the name of Jessica.

"Kade, this is your sister. Call me back as soon as possible," I said into my phone.

I exhaled deeply as I hung the phone up. I wanted to talk to Kade; I haven't heard from him since my father's funeral, and it was bothering me. I didn't care how he treated me. I loved him so much, and it just hurt that he didn't rock with me.

I couldn't even tell him about the money because he never answered his damn phone. I knew I couldn't cry over spilled milk simply because I was trying to excel in life. But, damn, I loved my baby brother.

I had just finished my morning run with Jessica, and I was feeling better and better as the days went by. Jessica had really shown me a better way of living. I was eating healthier, and I was on a strict no meat, no carbs diet, and only water for something to drink. It was working. My weight was dropping fast, and I was surprised by the woman standing before me.

"I am strong, I am beautiful, I got this"

"I am strong, I am beautiful, I am going to achieve my goals."

"I am strong, I am beautiful, I am free," I chanted, staring at my reflection in the full-length mirror in my bedroom.

That was the saying that Jessica taught me, and each and every time I recited it, I felt more and more confident. I was growing, and I could tell.

As I dressed in my bedroom, I couldn't help but stare at myself in the mirror. I was losing inches in my waist line, my thighs were toning up, and my smile was bright. I hadn't smiled like this in years, and it felt good.

A knock on my bedroom door startled me.

"Yes," I answered, and the door opened.

"Hey, love, are you ready?" she asked.

I glanced at myself one last time in the mirror and nodded before I grabbed my purse and was out the bedroom.

Me and Jessica hopped in her ride, and she took me to a dealership where I bought my first car with the money my father left me. I bought a 2017 Chevrolet Impala. It wasn't much, but it was everything to me. I didn't have many lessons with driving because I was a quick learner. I took two weeks of lessons, and then I was driving like it was nothing. It actually came natural to me.

"I love this," I squealed as we eyed my car. It was dope, and it was mine.

"Yes, it's nice. Now all we have to do is to take you to get your license. You wanna go for lunch after this?" Jessica asked me.

"Yeah, why not?" I chimed.

I was so busy looking at the car that I didn't pay attention to the voice ahead of me until he bumped into me as he passed by with a sales rep.

"Oh, I'm sorry." I looked up and was staring into the eyes of Prince, my twin brother, Knox's, best friend. I didn't even know he was out of jail.

"What's good, Mora?" He smiled at me, and my heartbeat increased.

Prince was so handsome.

"Hey, Prince, how you been?" I asked him.

"I've been good, baby girl. Tryna get me a new whip, ya know."

"I see. Me too." I smiled proudly.

"Oh yeah, I see that shit. That's a nice fit for you."

"Thanks." I chuckled.

"You heard from Knox?"

"Nah, he was supposed to call me. He gets out next week."

"Yeah, I know. If he calls you before he calls me, tell him to hit my line."

"Okay, will do! It was nice seeing you, Prince." I smiled as he bopped off from me.

"Oooohhh weeee, chile. Who was that?" Jessica asked, and I laughed.

"That was my brother's best friend. His name is Prince."

"Well, he's a cutie."

"Oh, gawdddd, Jessie." I giggled.

"I'm just saying, if he was little bit older, I would come for him, hunty," she joked, and we both laughed.

That's what I loved about Jessica. She was so damn real. I loved her caring personality.

Me and Jessica finished up at the car lot, but for some reason, I couldn't get Prince off my mind. He had grown into a man. He wasn't the same seventeen-year-old from high school, and it showed.

HOME SWEET HOME

KNOX

Stepping out of the prison gates, I stretched my arms above my head. The sun was shining brightly, and it was a slight breeze outside. The fresh air smelled good as shit to me right now. I'd been locked down for the last six years, and a nigga was finally free. I got out early due to good behavior and attending the GED program that they had. But, while I was in there, I demanded my respect. Niggas didn't fuck with me, and I made it known not to fuck with my niggas either.

I spotted the light blue Camry and a chick leaning against it. I smiled as I walked toward her. Once I got within arm's reach, I grabbed Gianna by her hips. Pulling her close to me, I kissed her lips roughly and brought my hands down to squeeze her ass.

"Damn, I'm happy to see you." She smiled at me as I pulled back from her.

"I'm happy to see yo fine ass too. What's up, baby?"

I eyed her thick thighs and protruding breasts that spilled out of her crop top.

"Nothing much. You ready?" she asked me.

"More than you know, man," I replied and walked around to the passenger side door then hopped inside her ride.

She started her car and pulled away from the jail. The ride back to Chicago was almost three hours, but it was one ride I was willing to take. It felt good to be out.

"So, whatchu wanna do first, baby?" she asked me, and I looked over at her.

Now what fucking kind of question is that?

"I wanna fuck," I boldly stated, and she giggled.

"You know I know that. I mean, like do you wanna eat or something?"

"I ain't tryna eat shit but you. I don't want nothing but some pussy all day after you take me to see my sister and lil brother," I told her, and she nodded.

I meant exactly what I said. A nigga had jacked off for the last few years, I need some wet wet on my dick ASAP.

Speaking of my little sister and brother, I hadn't heard from Kimora since the last letter I received from her when she told me Pops died. It had been three months since I received that later. It fucked me up that somebody killed my pops, but what a muthafucka didn't know was that they were gonna have to answer to me for the shit they pulled. My pops was a good dude, and for a muthafucka to take him out like it wasn't shit broke my soul. I had to remain strong because I was still behind those walls, but when not a soul wasn't looking, I let tears roll down my face. I couldn't take what the fuck these niggas did to my old man. He didn't deserve to go out like that.

Kimora told me she was living with some chick named Jessica, and I had to find her ASAP. I had a number on the letter that I was gonna call to see where my sis was. That lil nigga, Kade, wasn't shit, though. The man ain't tried to hit me up since I've been locked down. No letters, no visits, nothing. I didn't trip on it because he was young, but nah, fuck that, I was tripping.

That nigga Kade was 23 years old, and I still didn't know shit about him or where he was. He said fuck us, and I had a big problem with that shit.

"What's on yo mind, baby?" Gianna asked, snapping me from my train of thought.

"Nothing, just thinking about my people. Did you hear from my nigga Prince?"

"Yeah, him and my brother were over at my mom's a while ago playing cards and stuff," she said.

"Oh, okay. I need to ride on that nigga too," I said.

Prince had gotten out of jail six months before I did. He had received less time than me initially, but he stayed having fights in that bitch and going to the hole because he was labeled as a rapist. Word got out that he was in there because of rape, and by him being a pretty boy type, niggas were at his head. This shit was fucked up, though, because I believed my nigga when he said he didn't rape shawty.

I met Gianna through my nigga, Benz. Benz was the

nigga who helped me and Prince fight that day in the shower. After that day, Benz became like another brother to me. That was my nigga. Gianna was Benz's stepsister; her mother was married to his father. But they were cool as shit with each other. When we were locked down, he put me on to her. She was cool, and thick as hell in all the right places. She reminded me of Kimbella from *Love and Hip Hop*. She was riding for a nigga, and I couldn't wait to dig up in them guts.

I told her didn't wanna do the relationship shit exclusively because, to be honest, I was about to act a fool out in these streets. She was friend who I talked to over the phone, and I never asked her for shit. I didn't even ask her to pick me up from jail. She chose to do that shit, and I didn't mind it one bit.

Once we made it to the city, she headed toward the low end. She stayed in a condo in the Bronzeville area. When we got to her parking lot, my dick was already hard. Shit, a nigga was ready. I grabbed my shit out of her back seat, and we headed inside.

Going in her crib, it looked like the typical woman shit. Pink and white décor was in the living room, but I didn't give a fuck about that. I headed straight to the bedroom. I plopped down on the bed, and she looked at me seductively.

"What's up, Daddy?" she purred, and I eyed her.

"Give me a wash cloth. I need to shower again. I need to get this prison stench up off a nigga," I told her, and she complied.

When she came back, she handed me the wash cloth and

a dry towel, and I went in her bathroom. I looked for any traces of a nigga. Bitches were sneaky like that.

I started my shower and hopped inside. As I scrubbed my body, thoughts of fucking the shit out of Gianna when I was done ran through my mind. After showering, I hopped out, body still drenched, and headed in her bedroom butt ass naked.

Gianna was laid across the bed in only her red thong and red bra. I licked my lips as I eyed her body.

I crawled on the bed toward her and brought her to me. As I kissed her deeply, I climbed on top of her and spread her legs. She moaned in ecstasy as I kissed her neck and lightly sucked on it. I brought my hands up to her breast and fondled her nipples through the lace bra. I pulled her breast out and stuck one of them in my mouth. As I gently sucking on her nipple, she grabbed the back of my head.

"Ahh," she whispered in a low tone.

Removing her titty from my mouth, I slid down and pulled her panties off. I sniffed her pussy before I put my mouth on it. this was my first time with her, so I had to make sure that ass was smelling right. Once I was sure she was smelling right, I dived head first into her pussy, sucking on her clit and gently kissing the middle of her thighs. She clawed at my muscular back and moaned like crazy.

"Okay, baby! Okay!" she screamed when she couldn't take it anymore.

I got up and smirked as I looked down at her. Sweat glistening on her forehead as she stood up, and I motioned for her to turn that ass around. I stuck my dick in her, and she started going crazy as I pounded away, hitting all of her spots. I didn't know if the saying was true or not about that *fresh out of jail dick*, but I felt myself about to nut right away.

"Ahhhh, shitttt," I hissed as I pounded away in her pussy.

Her legs began to shake, and I couldn't help but smirk. Shit, it had been years since I felt some pussy, but a nigga still had it. I could feel my nut rising, and I put my hand around her neck. I pounded faster and faster, and she screamed like a damn mad woman. I closed my eyes because I wanted to relish in that shit.

"Ahhhh, fuck! Ahhhh, shit!" I growled as I sped my pace up, going faster and faster.

And as soon as I was about to cum, a voice startled me from the back, causing my dick to instantly go limp.

"Who the fuck is this nigga, Gianna?"

A big, lame ass nigga who looked like a broke down ass version snoop Dogg screamed. He was mad as hell, and I thought that shit was funny as fuck. I was standing there asshole naked and looking between him and his girl. If he thought I was gonna bitch up and run or some shit, then he had the right one because I didn't run from no nigga.

"Jake! Ba… Jake! Whatchu doing in my house?" she shouted while trying to find a blanket or some shit to cover herself.

I walked off toward the bathroom.

"Bitch, fuck you mean, what the fuck I'm doing here? I got keys, bitch! This my crib too! I pay the bills in this muthafucka, and you got some bitch ass nigga in here fucking you!" he shouted, and they started going back and forth.

I listened to them argue as I put on my shit. This was my first day out, and I couldn't afford to go back to jail. That shit just wasn't happening. A muthafucka wasn't about to take my peace from me. He could handle that bitch. I was mad as hell that I didn't get my nut off, but shit, I ain't gon' worry about it.

"Jake! I thought you were on the road! I'm sorry, baby!" she said, sounding pathetic.

I laughed to myself. I'd been talking on the phone and writing letters to Gianna for the longest. I knew that ass was too good to be true. I wasn't even mad, though. It wasn't like I loved the bitch.

After dressing, I walked out of her bathroom with my bag in tow. As I walked through her bedroom, Gianna and dude stopped arguing for a moment to look at me. I gave they asses a head nod and walked out of her bedroom.

When I got to her front door, her car keys were hanging on the wall. I debated if I should take her shit, and instead of doing the right thing, I did the wrong thing. I grabbed her car keys and left the crib. Outside, I hopped in her car and sped off.

I knew I needed a phone, so I went to the barber shop I used to go to. My old barber, who was more than happy to see a nigga, let me use his phone. I dialed the first number I knew off hand, and that was my nigga, Prince.

"Damnnn, sis, you outchea looking good as shit. Who the fuck is, this cause this ain't my Mora."

I smiled as I hugged Kimora for the third time. My twin was looking better than ever, and I damn sho was proud of her.

"Thanks, Bruh Bruh, I missed you so fucking much," she squealed, wrapping her hands around my neck and hugging me as tight as she could.

"I know, sis. I missed you too. So damn, Pops really ain't here, huh?" I said, even though I knew the answer.

A look of sadness washed over her face, and I could tell I had hit a sore spot. I mean, it was something that needed to be talked about anyway.

"Nah, he's not. But, you're here now, and that's all that matters."

When I called Prince at the barber shop, he came and scooped me right up. I called the number Kimora wrote on the letter she sent me, and some lady named Jessica answered and gave me her number. Now I was sitting out here at this fat ass house in country club hills and shit.

Prince was sitting over in the corner texting on his phone in his own lil world. The nigga had barely said two words to me since I hopped in his ride. I don't know who was occupying his time, but I wished the nigga would snap out of it. He hadn't been home for an entire year yet, and he was hooked on some bitch already. Damn shame.

"Damn, so whose crib is this?"

"This is Jessica's house." Kimora smiled proudly.

"It's dope as fuck"

"Exactly! It is the reason why I haven't moved yet." She giggled.

"Damn, sis, how you lose so much weight, if you don't mind me asking?"

I wanted to know. I wasn't trying to offend her, but Kimora looked good, she looked happy, and I liked what I saw on her face.

"Jessica helped me, Bruh Bruh. I was in a deep, dark depression when you went to jail, and after Daddy died, I was just lost. She helped me find my confidence, she helped me find my inner strength, and for that, I'll always be grateful for her."

I touched the side of her face where the scar was from when that bitch, Sierra, stabbed her, and she turned her head.

"Twin, you're still beautiful. That's lil shit to a giant, man."

"I know."

"Man, so what you had, surgery?" I asked with a raised eyebrow, and she cracked up laughing

"Hell no! I started watching what I eat, I exercise regularly, I run twice a day, once in the morning and once at night... well, jog. Shit, I ain't got to the point of running yet. And I've been trying this whole yoga and meditation thing. It works for me," she said, and I nodded.

Sitting in front of me was a totally different person from the last time I saw her. This was a person who stopped coming out of the house to now being confident as fuck, and I loved that shit about her.

"Well, damn. Lil sis done grew up on me," I said, and she giggled.

"K, stop it! You act like I'm a size two or some shit. I'm

still considered plus sized and curvy. I wear a size 12/14 now. It's not much, but I'm proud of my change because coming from where I was, I feel better about myself."

"Man, I love this shit. I don't give a fuck if you were the same way, as long as I'm back with you," I told her.

"Where Kade lil bitch ass at?" I growled, speaking on my lil brother.

"I haven't heard from Kade since Daddy's funeral and that's been months ago. He doesn't even know I got something for him, but I refuse to give to him because he doesn't fuck with us."

"Wait, whatchu got for us? And when did you start cursing like that?" I eyed her.

"I started cursing like this after living with a devil named Candice, and what I got for you, you don't even now the half. I'm glad it's early because we about to go shopping, brother." She smiled, and my frown turned into a smile.

Kimora grabbed my hand, and we got up to walk out the door. I tapped Prince on his shoulder and told him he could bounce, and I'll get up with him later. Mora had a whip and every fucking thing. She was pushing a 2017 Dodge Impala. Shit wasn't a Benz, but that bitch was nice as fuck.

Kimora drove me to the mall, and the first thing she got me was a cell phone from the Verizon wireless store. I got the Samsung Galaxy 8 because that iPhone shit was too fucking complicated. I wasn't in the mood to be fucking with that shit.

Next place we hit up was DTLR, True Religion, and Jimmy Jazz. I got a couple pairs of sneakers from Footlocker. Afterward, we went to the dealership. I picked out a cocaine white Dodge Charger. That bitch was wet. I was in love with that muthafucka already.

Kimora still hadn't told me where she got this bread from. I figured the chick, Jessica, gave it to her because she was a lawyer and all that shit. I didn't drive it, though, due to me not having my license just yet. So, we got the whip shipped to Jessica's crib.

After it was all said and done, me and Kimora ended up at Olive Garden having dinner. I had taste for some pasta. I wanted something fast and quick. I still hadn't figured out where I was gonna lay my head tonight, but the way I was feeling, I didn't give a fuck where I laid at. It just felt good to be home.

"Twin, so what's good? Where you getting all this money and shit from?"

"Daddy," she replied.

"Whatchu mean Daddy?"

"Daddy left us some money, Knox. He had paper. I mean a whole lot of paper," she said, and my eyes bucked.

"You fucking lying."

"Nah, I'm not."

Kimora smiled and started fumbling in her purse. She pulled out her wallet and went in it. Moments later, she came out with a bank card and handed it to me.

"What's this?"

"It's your bank card with your money in your account, Knox. You need to go and get your state ID before you can just walk in a bank and tell them to give you money and shit." She laughed.

"Lil nigga, I know what I gotta do."

"And your pin number is our birthday. You can always change it, but I used something that would be easily remember."

"Aight, bet. Aye, Mora, thank you for everything you did for me today. Damn, sis, I missed you, and it feels really good to be back home."

"Bruh Bruh, you don't have to worry about anything. Daddy leaving us that money was a way for us to start over, and all I wanna do is leap out on faith and restart my life. You've always had my back, and its only right that I have yours," she said, and I nodded.

I didn't know how much the account held, but I was grateful for whatever the fuck it was.

"Damn, so this Jessica chick is cool, huh?"

"Yes, I love her so much. She has been the mother I've never had, she's been there for me in ways you can't imagine. She gave me hope and showed me there's a way to make it. She also showed me there's a way to believe in yourself. I'm stronger now because of her"

"Yeah, man, I see that. Shid, I'm gonna have to get ole Jesse a gift or something," I said, and Mora cracked up laughing.

"You so silly. So, where you staying at tonight?" she asked me, and I shrugged.

"Shit, I don't know. I thought I was gonna be crashing with this lil shawty, but that don't seem like it's happening," I said, thinking about Gianna's special ass.

"Well, I can get you a room, and we can figure out a way to find you a place."

"I can't afford no rent, sis. I gotta get on my hustle first."

"Bruh Bruh, you must not be understanding what I'm saying to you. You don't ever have to fucking work. Daddy made sure we were fucking good. Literally. We have money to blow, and I'm saying that in the humblest way that I can."

"If that's the case, why you still living with Jessica?"

"Because… I'm scared to be alone, K," she said in a sad tone, and I understood.

"Aight, well the ball is in your court, sis. You can get me right. I'm just gonna follow yo lead," I told her, and she smiled.

"I'm glad because I wanna decorate everything, and I want my own room at your place too." She grinned, and I chuckled.

This shit was the best homecoming gift I could've ever received. I didn't know the exact amount my father left us, but whatever it was, I was grateful for it. I wasn't gonna ask Kimora for any of the money I was gonna let her handle all the business, and whatever she gave me, I was just gonna roll with it. Money and all, I still needed something to do with my time.

Kimora and I chopped it up over drinks and more food, and then my new cell rang. Nobody had this number but Benz and Prince. I looked down, and it was Prince calling me. Shit felt like old times.

"What's good, broski?" I answered.

"Shit much, nigga, we about to hit up the strip club. You riding?" he asked me.

"Yeah, y'all gotta come and scoop me, though. I'm about to check into the Hilton hotel on Michigan avenue," I told him.

"Aight, bet. We gonna call you when we get there."

"Ask that nigga where the fuck is my car before his bitch ass be back in jail!"

I heard Gianna's voice in the background, and I laughed, causing Kimora to look at me strangely. Shit, I almost forgot about her ride. I left that shit at the barber shop when I had Prince come and get me.

"Tell her to go grab her shit from Dexter's shop," I said while laughing, and Prince laughed as well.

"Nigga, yo ass wild. But, aye, text my phone when you check into your room," he said.

I agreed and hung up the phone.

Tonight, I was about to see some ass and titties. My first day out had been one to remember, and I was gonna end this bitch with a bang.

I'M GROWN NOW

SPIRIT

"Come on, Mama, get back on the bed," I urged my mother, who constantly fought with me.

Whenever it was time for her to lie down, she always tried this bullshit. It was frustrating to say the least. I loved my momma with everything in me, but I was tired now.

I pushed the covers back, and she climbed in the bed. I covered her up, and she smiled at me lovingly. My mother had officially lost her mind. Her medication didn't even work anymore. Now I just gave her pills the doctors prescribed to keep her calm.

My father died three years ago, and I had to come home from school to take care of my mom. My life hasn't been easy ever since I could remember, and as time goes on, it seems like it only gets worse.

After covering my mother up, I went upstairs to my bedroom and entered the bathroom. I hopped in the shower and thought about my life and how it had gone down the drain. Things I did in my past came back to bite me in the ass. It put a halt on my dreams, and I was the only one to blame. I should've been a phycologist right now in grad school, but instead, I was a nurse for my ailing mother. I should've been partying, traveling, living life, but instead I was working to pay bills for a house, not an apartment, but a fucking house, all because I didn't want my parents' house to go to the bank. This was the house I grew up in. I couldn't see my mom's challenging work go down the drain like that. I also didn't want my mother in a mental institution. I knew I could take care of her better than anyone else could.

After showering, I put my clothes on for work and looked myself over in the full-length mirror in my bedroom. I'd grown to be such a beautiful woman with a lot of scars and a lot of regret.

I walked out of my bedroom and peeked in on my mom one last time before I left out the front door. The minute I walked out of my front door. I stopped in my tracks as I saw the figure leaning against my car.

"Tyree, really?" I exclaimed, looking at my ex-boyfriend who was leaning against my car and smoking a blunt.

I met Tyree my first year of college; he was something new and fresh in my life, but he was a hot damn mess. He stayed messing with bitches, and I just couldn't take it anymore.

"This is what I gotta do to talk to you now? I gotta stalk you and shit, huh?" he asked as I moved closer to my car.

I rolled my eyes because I didn't feel like going through the motions with Tyree right now. Tonight, wasn't a good night for me.

"Tyree, I gotta go, and we ain't got shit to talk about. Go talk to that bitch I caught you with," I snapped as I open the driver's side door.

"Man, that's some bullshit, Spirit, and you know it. That shit wasn't anything. Shit ain't mean shit to me. I keep telling you that. I fucked up, Spirit, damn."

"That's the whole point, Tyree, you always fucking up and I ain't in the mood for it no more. I've forgiven you more times than I should have. Now move because I gotta get to work."

"Spirit, what I gotta do for you to talk to me? Baby, give me another chance. I promise I'm gonna make this shit right."

"Tyree, call me in the morning, but tonight I don't wanna talk. I'm not having a good night as it is already, sooo please don't make it worse," I explained and closed the driver's side door.

I didn't give him another chance to say anything else as I started my car and peeled away from the house. I had too much shit on my mind to be dealing with his ass.

When I pulled up to my job, I exhaled deeply. *Here we go,* I thought as I got out of my car and headed for the backdoor entrance.

Entering the club, the bouncers all spoke to me as I made my way to my dressing room. I went in the dressing room and plopped down at the vanity mirror. I looked at my face, and tears clouded the brim of my eyes. I never wanted to do this shit, but this shit paid the bills. I made the money quick, and it was easy for me to stack.

A knock on my dressing room door caused me to wipe my eyes with the back of my hand.

"Who is it?" I chimed.

"It's Cream," my home girl said, and a smile graced my face.

"Come in, boo."

The door opened, and my homegirl, Cream, came inside. She was wearing a two-piece hot pink thong and hot pink tassels on her breasts with a cow girl hat and some cow girl boots on.

"What's up, boo? They out there waiting for you." She smiled and gave me a hug.

"Chile, I know. I'm just not ready... I'm tired Cream," I exhaled, and she gave me a look of sorrow.

"Sis, once you got yo money stacked, leave this shit alone. But you a headliner now, Desire," Cream said, calling me by my stage name.

"I know what I am, and I hate it, but this shit pays the bills anyway. How's it looking out there?" I asked.

"Girl, it's cool. Light crowd for it to be a Thursday." She shrugged, and I nodded my head.

I applied my burgundy lipstick to my lips and stood up from the vanity. I walked over to the small dresser that was in the room and pulled out my fishnet top and my neon orange thong. I placed the 6-inch sparkly pumps on my feet, and my long hair was brushed into a tight pony tail. Staring at myself in the mirror, I couldn't help but think about how bad I looked. How I was a bad bitch but a sad bitch all at the same time.

I couldn't believe I resorted to becoming a fucking stripper. After all the things I'd been through and leaving school, stripping was the one thing I could do. I met Cream, at my college, and she's been working at *Infatuation* for a long ass time. She was the one who told me about the club when she knew I was down on my luck.

I started there two years ago, and man, when I say it's been a rollercoaster ride, I'm not gonna lie. But I worked my way up, and men only came in there to see me. I didn't do regular dances; I only worked the VIP room and the stage. After that, I usually left there on a good night with about three G's in my pocket.

Once I was done dressing and shit, I left my dressing room with Cream following me. Me and Cream did sets together, so it wasn't awkward for us to be on the stage together. I stood behind the stage and connected eyes with the DJ. He knew that was his cue to play my song that I had chosen for the day. I always put on a performance when I went out on the stage. That's how I got so popular. I was a good dancer, so it came naturally.

When I got on the stage, my mind went to a different place. I was no longer Spirit. I was Desire, and my job was to entice. That's it. I was going for a slower vibe today. I wasn't in the mood to be throwing my ass in so many circles that it felt like I was gonna break my fucking back. Tonight, I went a little old school with it. I chose this song because of the way Trey Songz sings it.

"Welcome to my sex room. Where your body meets my body,

it's our private after party. If you want it girl I got in my sex room. Candles and Pole sets your body to your soul, sex room, from the bed to the floor. Sex room, mirrors in the head board, even got a camcorder, baby won't you dance in my sex room. Welcome to my sex room, here your body meets my body, it's a private afterparty, if you want it girl, I got it. In my sex room."

I grinded my body up and down the pole, doing splits, and slowly popping my ass.

I got on my hands and knees and crawled to the edge of the stage to make eye contact with the crowd. Doing this shit, I learned how to be a seductress. Niggas were throwing money on the stage, and some were sticking bills in my garter.

Once I made my way around all corners of the stage engaging with the men and even some of the women. When I got to the last corner of the stage my eyes bucked at the two faces I was seeing. It has been years since I've seen either one of them. My heart started to race, and my hands got clammy. Knox and Prince. Lord knows if it wasn't another awkward moment in my life this was it right now.

Knox smirked at me, and Prince had a surprised expression on his face. I never forgot what me and Prince did back in the day. Shit, I couldn't forget if I wanted to. But, seeing him now made my heart rate increase tremendously. Knox was still as fine as he was the day he left and went to prison, but this time, he was a grown ass man. I was confused as fuck right now. I moved away from their corner and started dancing again in the middle of the stage.

It felt like I was dancing off cue because my mind was too filled with other shit. My shit ran rampant as I thought about Knox and Prince still being friends and still hanging together. And how I still wanted the both of them in the worst way.

AFTER MY SET WAS OVER, I RACED TO THE BACK WHERE THE dressing rooms were located. I quickly changed my outfit and stuffed my money in my bag. Fuck it, I wasn't gonna even do the VIP lounge tonight. I couldn't stand to be in the building any longer knowing that the both of them were there.

After dressing, I made my way out of the dressing room, and as I was about to head to the front of the club, someone grabbed me by my elbow. I started to yell, but I looked into the hazel eyes of Prince fine ass. He was still fine as shit after all these years.

"Prince..."

"What's up, Spirit?" He smiled at me.

"Nothing, just uhhhh, working as you can see." I let out a nervous chuckle. I didn't know what to say to him at this moment.

"I see. Man, I could never imagine this is the shit you was doing though." He eyed me, and I frowned.

Who the fuck was he to sit back and judge me? He didn't have a fucking clue what the fuck I've been through in my life. As matter of fact, he knew what I was going through.

"I could've never imagined you would rape somebody," I shot back.

The look on his face wiped my smirk away.

"Damn, so we getting hostile with each other. I haven't seen you in years. I've called, and you never answered. I don't think this is a good way to start off."

"What are we starting off, Prince? We fucked once, and it was a mistake. Also, I don't want a man. I got other shit on my mind."

"And I ain't tryna be yo' man, Spirit. We had a friendship back in the day before we did anything sexual, but if you don't want either, then shit, cool with me. I was just tryna see how yo ass been. I mean, my moms said you ain't came by to visit in years. So that says a lot."

I swallowed hard when he said that. I had kept up with Prince through his mother, and some things are better off left alone when you're moving forward in your life.

"Prince, it wasn't like that," I tried to explain, but he held his hand up to stop me.

"It is what it is, ma. I was just coming to rap with you. That's it. It's clear you ain't tryna hear a nigga right now, and I get it."

"Prince, I'm sorry. I don't wanna come off as a bitch to you. I swear I don't. I stopped coming around your mom because it was just too hard for me. I couldn't stomach what had happened to you. And then my mother was getting sicker and sicker as the days went by."

"I get all of that shit you saying, Spirit. But I would've been a friend to you nonetheless. I've always been a friend to you regardless of us fucking or not."

He was right. Back in the day when I needed someone or anything, Prince always had my back. I felt like I turned my back on him when I went to college.

"Your right, Prince, and I'm sorry about that," I told him.

He just stared at me, and I moved away from his gaze. The shit was intimidating. His cell started to ring, and he pulled it out.

"Here I come, bro," he spoke into the phone.

"I gotta go. It was good seeing you, Spirit."

"Yeah, you too," I replied.

As I watched him walk away, nervous jitters ran through my body. I tried to wrap my mind around the conversation me and Prince just had. Fighting back tears, I made my way to the front of the club. Listening the harsh reality of your situation will make you sick to the stomach.

As I made my way to the front, I spotted Prince talking to a dude with long dread locs. I was looking for Knox, but I didn't see him anywhere. I left the club, and as I started walking toward the parking lot, I spotted Knox talking to some guys we knew from around the way. We connected eyes, and I swallowed hard. I couldn't even think of anything to say to him.

"Aye, Spirit. Wait up, though," he said.

I stopped walking, and he walked up on me with a smile on his face.

"What's good, shawty?" he asked, looking me up and down.

I sort of blushed. Knox still had that same effect on me.

"You tell me what's good. How you been, Knox?" I asked.

"I'm good. I just got out today." He smiled proudly.

"Oh yeah? Well, I'm glad you're home. Have a good

night," I said and tried to walk away, but he stopped me in my tracks.

"Aye, where the fuck you going, though? I wasn't done talking to you," he said.

I frowned at his choice of words.

"Knox, maybe you've been gone too fucking long, but I don't know who you think you talking to like that," I snapped.

He burst into laughter, which caused me to smile.

"I'm just fucking with you, shawty."

"Un huh, whatever, nigga," I said, and he placed his arm around my shoulder as we started moving toward the parking lot.

I could smell the Remy on his breath, and I knew without a doubt that he was drunk as a skunk.

"Man, so what happened to my good girl that I wanted all those years ago?" he said, and I didn't say anything.

"You don't hear me talking to you, Spirit?" he said in a low tone, his breath tickling my earlobe and causing tingles to make my pussy throb.

"I hear you, Knox. Life happened to this good girl."

"I know. What's up, though? You gonna let a nigga get yo number this time around or what?" he asked as we stood in front of my car.

"Yeah, I think can do that, Knox."

"This time around, we gon' make some shit happen. Maybe put a baby or two in yo thick ass," he said, and I chuckled.

"This time around." I smiled as I rattled off my number and he punched it into his Galaxy phone.

"Yeah, this time around. Shit, you grown now," he said.

"Bitch, you still shaking yo ass at this muthafucking club?" a familiar voice shouted.

I looked behind me, and Tyree was walking fast as hell toward me and Knox. My heart started to pound in my chest because I knew how much of a clown Tyree's ass could be.

"Tyree... Gone somewhere with that drama," I said to him, but he wasn't hearing it.

"Nah, bitch, that's why you ain't tryna fuck back with a nigga. 'Cause you never stopped working at this club. Who this fuck is this clown ass nigga?" he said, addressing Knox.

Knox stood there with a stone expression on his face. Tyree went on and on until Knox knocked the shit out of him, causing Tyree to hit the concrete with a thud. He instantly went to sleep. I looked down at Tyree and then at Knox who bore a smirk on his face.

"Ma, make sure you use that number, so you can see what it's like to fuck with a real nigga. These goofies ain't cutting it, Spirit," he said and kissed my cheek.

He walked away, and I got in my car. I peeled away, leaving Tyree's dumb ass on the ground. *Dumb ass nigga.* The whole drive back to my house, I couldn't get Knox off my mind. I needed to talk to Prince ASAP because Knox could never know what went down between us. I wanted to leave the past in the past. Damn, I was glad he was back home.

NIGGAS GOT ME FUCKED UP

PRINCE

"**A**ye, man, you knew shawty on that stage? She bad as fuck," my nigga, Benz, said as I watched the stripper Cream who was in front of us shaking her ass.

"Yeah, that's my homie from back in the day."

I couldn't help but think about Spirit. She still looked the same, just more mature now. I felt some type of way that she just brushed a nigga off like I wasn't shit. She thought I was still checking for her, but I wasn't. I didn't want Spirit in that manner, but damn, I thought we were homies. We fucked back in the day, and one thing led to another, then both of our lives spun out of control.

For her to be so standoffish to a nigga was uncalled for. Fuck her, though. I didn't understand how she succumbed to being a fucking stripper. That wasn't like her at all. I thought

Spirit had gone to do great things, but I guess not. My cell vibrated in my pocket, and I went inside to grab it. I looked at the caller and I let out a deep sigh. It was Dana calling me.

Dana was one of my mother's church going friends' daughter. I met her when I got out, and I was so thirsty for some fucking pussy that I was jumping at anything that came my way. I know y'all probably thinking that I should've learned my fucking lesson from the last time that shit that got me sent to jail. But, fuck that, a nigga was horny, and I was fresh out.

My mother thought it would be a good idea if I met a good girl who had her head on her shoulders. And, yeah, Dana was financially stable and all that other shit, but that good girl act she tried to portray in front of my mama and the church went out the window once she was bussing it open for a nigga after only three days. I was feeling Dana, but not like that. I ain't want a girl in my life. I was too busy trying to get my shit in order.

That jail shit fucked a nigga's head up. It got out that I was in jail for rape, and muthafuckas were coming at me left and right. I stayed in the hole for knocking niggas' shit loose in that bitch. They thought 'cause a nigga was light skinned and had curly hair that I was some type of bitch. Pussy ass niggas had the right one. I was a beast with these hands, and I learned early how to use a shank. Eventually, muthafuckas got the picture, and they fell the fuck back.

I didn't do all my years in the joint with Knox. He had gotten transferred, so once he was gone, I only had myself and my nigga Benz. But niggas knew not to fuck with me. I had proven myself time and time again.

"Aye, bro, who them niggas right there?" Benz asked me.

I turned to the doorway to see my oldest brother, Terror, and his crew walking through the doors. I frowned when I saw this nigga. I couldn't stand my oldest brother, but no one really knew how I felt about him. Terror wasn't shit, and he was just that, a fucking terrorist on these streets he was forty-one years old. He didn't even fuck with our moms. I was glad he didn't, though. My mom didn't need that type of stress or drama that the nigga brought every time he came around.

"That's my brother," I said.

"Word, nigga?" Benz asked me.

"Yeah, man." I shrugged and turned back around to gaze at the stripper.

"Yooooo, ain't that Knox lil brother he told me to get at while he was locked down?" he asked.

I had gotten irritated with Benz asking questions and shit, but I turned back around to see Kade, who was Knox's little brother, with Terror and his crew. Lo and behold, the bitch ass nigga, Trey, was with them as well. Looking like a bunch of fucking followers. Me and Terror connected eyes, and he came toward me. I didn't feel like talking to this nigga right now. I was down and out, and this bitch ass nigga wouldn't even help me out when I was locked down. He wouldn't even help my moms pay her bills or none of that shit.

One thing about me, I was a nigga determined to make something happen. I had only been out for six months, but three months in, I had connected with these niggas by the name of the Billions. This nigga Javier had the purest white in the Chi. He was top muthafucking dog, and I felt like my own man since I didn't have to work for Terror. I worked for my muthafucking self.

Benz knew some niggas who were in good with the Billions, and Javier gave us some work on consignment. Within in a month, I flipped that shit and made double. I was able to pay him back and re up all at the same time. I wasn't some rich ass nigga like my brother, but I was making shit happen in these streets. I didn't need a squad; it was only me, Benz, and his little brother, Tony. We were fucking the southside and eastside up. Money was coming in, and I was starting to get nervous.

When niggas knew you were in the streets making money, they trigger fingers started to itch. Wanna stick muthafuckas up and shit. And I know what y'all probably thinking, why a muthafuckas wait until they were good in their 20's to start selling drugs? Well, the answer is simple. I was living at my momma's crib, and I was sick of it already. Fuck that, a nigga needed his own. I had responsibilities and shit that I had to take care of.

This was the only way to get some easy money. Some might say I was an overnight success for how well I've been doing, but selling drugs ain't rocket science. You find a couple of fiends, and if you got that good shit, they keep coming back and word gets around that you the nigga to see.

"Yeah, that's him. Where that nigga Knox at anyway?" I said, looking around and not seeing Knox in view anywhere.

"Shit, I don't know. I saw that nigga leave out talking to some niggas from his neighborhood or some shit like that."

Benz waved the waitress over and ordered another bottle

of Henny. I couldn't take my eyes off my brother and his entourage. This nigga Terror was something else. They all walked over into the VIP area and sat around buying bottles and shit. Me and Terror connected eyes, and he smirked then responded by giving me a head nod. I didn't say shit. I watched as he got out of his seat and came my way. I took a deep breath and exhaled sharply.

Once he was up on me, he extended his hand for a handshake, and I just looked at it.

"Prince, it's disrespectful to not acknowledge someone when they're speaking to you," he said.

I looked at him and chuckled.

"What's good, bruh?"

"Shit much, little brother. How have you been?"

"I'm good. I'm maintaining, you know what I mean."

"Yeah… I'm glad you're out."

"I am too."

"How's Mama?" he asked me, and I chuckled again.

"She's good."

"Oh, aight. So, I want you to come by my office at the car wash in the morning. I wanna holla at you about some things," he said, and I laughed.

"Nah. I'm good, homie."

"Is that right?" He eyed me.

"That's right."

"I heard you out here fucking with them Billions brothers?"

"You heard right."

"I see you good at this drug dealing shit. So, how about we talk?"

"I guess I am. But as I said before, no need to talk. I'm good."

"I see, I see. Well, I'll see you around, little brother." He smirked, and before he walked off, he leaned in close and whispered in my ear.

"Lil nigga, the next time you leave my hand hanging in thin air, I'm gonna show you the reason the streets call me terror. Blood or not. Disrespect is a death wish," he whispered, and I smirked

"Whatever you say, Big Brother," I replied.

He smiled, patted my shoulder, and walked off. Terror's old ass was over forty years old and he acted as if he was still in his prime. The muthafucka needed his ass beat something good. Out here terrorizing these streets. Me and Terror were seventeen years apart. I told my moms she had to be something special to have a baby seventeen years after the first one.

I was so busy with thoughts of Terror and Spirit that I didn't see when Knox ran into the VIP area and squared up with that bitch ass nigga Trey until I heard all the commotion.

"Aye, nigga, that's Knox," Benz said as he ran to the VIP. area with me right behind him.

Knox had Trey's bitch ass hemmed up against the couch, and this nigga Kade started swinging on his own brother. I tossed the lil nigga to the side, and all the niggas that were in Terror's crew started throwing blows. We were picking up liquor bottles, and the club went into pandemonium. We were knocking niggas the fuck out.

Security tried to come in and break shit up, but they only made things worse. The next thing I knew...

Boom, Boom, Boom.

Gun shots rang out, and niggas started to scatter. I grabbed Knox by the back of his shirt, and we raced to the front of the club. Too many folks were tryna get out, so I picked up a chair and threw it into the glass, breaking that shit. Me and my niggas went out that big ass window in front of the club.

We raced to the parking lot and hopped in my ride. I started my ignition and peeled off fast as fuck.

"Whewwww!! Nigga, LET'S GO! LET'S Go!" Knox shouted from the back seat.

The nigga was in charge mode, and I had to laugh at his ass.

"Shid, my first day out wasn't nearly this exciting," I said, and we all laughed.

"Man, I told y'all when I see that lil nigga, Trey, it was gonna be on sight for his goofy ass. He thought I was letting it ride what he did to my lil sister. I wasn't letting that shit ride," Knox snapped, and I totally understood.

Shit, Kimora's ass was fucking gorgeous when I saw her earlier today. I had to pretend like I was so busy in my phone, so I wouldn't be trying to be all up in her shit. I knew Knox wouldn't have agreed to that shit. The nigga was very overprotective when it came to his sister, and I understood. But, damn, Kimora was bad as fuck. She lost weight; it wasn't drastic, but the weight she did lose enhanced her already there curves. Man, when I say her ass so fucking fat, it didn't make any sense. And that long ass hair was plus.

"Man, what the fuck is up with your lil brother, bro?" Benz asked Knox, and I wanted to know the same thing.

I didn't understand how Kade could go against the grain.

"Man, I don't know what the fuck is up with the lil nigga, but I promise you after today, I'm cutting his ass the fuck off," Knox spewed angrily.

"Nah, man, you know he's young... He still playing follow the leader behind Trey's bitch ass." I scoffed just thinking about it.

"Man, I don't give a fuck what he's playing. He needs to get his shit in order 'fore his ass be dead out here fucking with these clown ass niggas. I promise I'm gon' put that lil nigga, Trey, in the dirt."

"Nigga, you must be trying to go back to the joint?" I looked at him through the rearview mirror, and he smirked.

"Nigga, it ain't like I ain't never been before."

"Shut the fuck up, man. Where I'm dropping you off to?" I asked him.

"Nigga, the Hilton on Michigan Avenue. I'm drunk as fuck though, bro, and I'm glad I had a good coming home party." His voice slurred, and I shook my head. This nigga was too drunk.

"Bro, that wasn't yo coming home party, muthafucka," Benz added, and we all started laughing.

"Shidddd, nigga, it felt like it." He laughed.

I dropped my niggas off. and then I dialed up Dana. She answered on the first ring and told me she's been waiting on me.

When I pulled up to her spot, I went in her crib and headed straight for her bedroom. Walking in the bedroom, my eyes bucked at what I saw. It was a chick in the bedroom with her head between Dana's legs. She was eating her pussy, and Dana was moaning.

"Hey, baby, I've... I've been waiting on you." She moaned, and I smiled.

I told y'all this church girl shit she wanted to pull wasn't shit but façade. Dana was a certified freak, but I loved that shit, though. I stripped out of my clothes and hopped in the bed with them.

I'M COMING FOR EVERYTHING

KIMORA

Ring, ring, ring. I looked over on my nightstand and grabbed my cell phone. It was going on 6:00 in the morning, and I didn't have a clue as to who this could be calling me. I started not to answer, but the caller was persistent.

"Hello?" I answered.

"He-Hello?" a chick's small voice came through the phone. It seemed as if she was crying.

"Hello, who is this?" I asked, sitting up in bed because now I was on high alert.

"My name is Nisa, and I know you don't know me, but I know you. I'm calling about Kade. He... He was my boyfriend. And I'm at St. Bernard hospital and he... he just died." She broke down crying and tears rushed to my eyes.

"What? Are you sure?" I don't know why I asked that dumb ass question, but I did.

"Huh?"

"Look, I'm sorry, but I'm on my way right now. Please... please stay there," I instructed her, and she agreed.

I hopped out of bed and ran out my room. I knocked on Jessica's bedroom door, and when she opened it, she was fully dressed. I knew she was on her way to work.

"Oh my God. What's wrong, Mora?" she asked with a face full of concern.

"They killed my little brother," I cried as I broke down in her arms.

I was sick and tired off grieving. I never gave him his share of the money, and I never got back in touch with him after Daddy's funeral. I felt so fucked up about everything.

"Don't cry, sweetie. Let's get to the hospital. Did you call Knox?" she asked me, and that's when a lightbulb went off in my head.

I forgot to call Knox.

"No, I didn't. Let me call him now," I said with shaky hands as I went in the bedroom and grabbed my cell phone.

I dialed up Knox, and he didn't answer, which I knew he wouldn't. He was a hard sleeper, but years in jail should've broken that. I called back to back at least 10 times and still no answer.

I decided I would try later and that I needed to get to the hospital to see about Kade. I dressed in haste and made my way to the hospital. When I got there, I walked inside, and I didn't know where to go. I spotted a light skinned chick with a short haircut leaned against the wall with her arms folded, and she looked sad. I took out my phone as I stared at her and dialed her number. I saw her look down at her phone, and she was about to answer it, but I hung up. I walked up on her and called her name

"Nisa?" I eyed her, and she had the most beautiful dark green eyes.

"Hey. Kimora?"

"Yeah, that's me."

"I'm… I'm so sorry… I'm so sorryyy." She bawled her eyes out, and I was stuck.

What was she sorry about? What happened? How did my brother die?"

Tears fell from my eyes as she cried. I brought her into my arms and hugged her tightly. Although I didn't know the whole story about how Kade got killed, we both needed to be strong in order to find out everything that happened.

When the doctor came out, he told me that Kade sustained three gunshot wounds to the head. I was confused. Just as the doctor was finishing up his last statement, Knox called me back.

"Hello?"

"What good, twin?" he asked in a groggy voice.

"Knox… Kade got killed last night," I said just above a whisper.

"What? What the fuck you just say, Mora?" he barked, and my tears started to flow again.

Hearing the anger in voice and the hurt that laced it broke me down.

"He's gone, Knox. Somebody killed him last night. He

was shot three times," I told him with the words feeling like venom flowing from my mouth.

I told Knox what hospital we were at, and he took an Uber up there. When he walked into the hospital, I could see the pain all over his face. I told hm what the doctor said and introduced him to Nisa, Kade's girlfriend. He broke down just like that. In all my years of living, I've never seen Knox cry the way he did. We were heartbroken. We now had to bury another family member, and after today, I didn't think our lives will ever be the same.

SITTING IN THE RECEPTION HALL AT KADE'S REPAST, MY MIND couldn't stop wondering about my little brother. He had done so many things that I didn't even know he was into. He was working for this dude name Terror, who I had yet to meet. Nisa told me a lot of things about Kade. Things I never could have imagined he was into. All in all, it made me want more answers.

Knox told me it was shots fired when the fight happened at the strip club that night, but Nisa said that Kade's body was found on the southside in an alley. They left him there to die, and I had a big problem with it. I was sick and fucking tired of muthafuckas coming for my family and taking advantage of them.

"What's good, Mora?" Knox's friend Prince said to me as he took a seat beside me.

I looked over at him, and he smiled.

"Hey, Prince. What's up?"

"How you feeling?" he asked, and I sort of frowned.

"Feeling like the world wants to destroy me," I said, and his eyes widened.

"Why you say that shit, ma?" he asked.

"Because when am I going to catch a fucking break? I just buried my lil brother! When is this shit going to end? I can't take it," I snapped, and he just stared at me intently.

"Man, I'm sorry about what happened to Kade. He didn't deserve that shit. He was good kid. We all know that shit, but when you run with the big dogs, there are consequences, and every action has them," he said, and I nodded.

I heard what he was saying, but honestly, I didn't wanna hear that shit. I was just fucking tired of it.

"You ain't listening to me, ma, but I just wanted to check up on you and see if you good," he said and kissed my cheek before he got out of the chair and walked away.

My eyes zoomed in on the crew that was walking through the front doors of the hall. It was an older dude and an entourage of younger cats behind him. My mind wondered who the fuck was that, and what the fuck were they doing there. I spotted Trey's bitch ass, and I hopped out of my chair. Oh no. I didn't give a flying fuck who he was with. He had to fucking go.

I marched over to the crowd and stood in front of them.

"Get the fuck out!" I shouted to Trey.

The few guests that we did have stopped and watched the commotion that was going on.

"Fat ass Mora done got thick," Trey said, and I frowned.

"Get the fuck out! Get the fuck out right now, you bitch ass nigga!!" I screamed again.

I hated this nigga Trey. I wished nothing but bad on his bitch ass. He was part of the reason why I was so fucked up mentally. But no more. I was not gonna allow any of these muthafuckas to make me feel anything less that important. Fuck that! I was tired of these muthafuckas.

When Trey bitch ass didn't move, I knew what to do next.

"KNOXXXXXXXXXXXX!!" I screamed my brother's name so loud.

I knew once he saw Knox, he was gonna hightail it the fuck out of there. His smirk turned into a frown, and the older dude who was standing there never moved an inch. He just stared at me with a smirk on his face.

"Sweetheart, can I talk to you for a second?" the older cat asked me.

I was mugging the fuck out of Trey bitch ass and still wondering at the same time where the fuck was Knox.

"We ain't got shit to talk about," I snapped at the older dude, and he chuckled.

"A feisty lil thing, huh?" he said and grabbed my hand.

I looked up at him, and for him to be an older dude, he was super handsome. He had a salt and pepper goatee, chocolate skin, a bald head, and the Armani suit he had on made him look dapper. He had swag that you couldn't deny. The Hermes cologne he wore was intoxicating. I tried to snatch my hand away, but he held a firm grip on it.

"I'm not feisty, but I don't like trash, and that's exactly what Trey is." I rolled my eyes, and the dude laughed.

"Aye, Trey, she wants you gone, so leave, lil nigga," he announced while looking at me.

Trey didn't say a word as he mugged me and walked out. This nigga had some clout, and I liked that shit.

"Dismiss! Pay ya respects to the family and bounce," he told the rest of his crew, and they left from behind him.

I watched as they all placed something in the grieve basket that was on a table, even though we didn't need the money or anything. Jessica suggested that I put the basket out because sometimes people liked to bring the family cards and stuff of that nature.

"You're too beautiful to be so feisty." The older dude smiled at me.

"Thanks." I blushed and looked away.

I hadn't ever had a dude look at me like that nor tell me I was beautiful.

"Shid, I should be thanking you for gracing me with your beauty," he cracked, and it was sort of corny to me. He still held on to my hand, and I was wondering why.

"Can I have my hand back?" I eyed him, and he looked at me he kissed the back of my hand. Then slowly, he let my hand go.

"Can I call you sometime, Kimora?" he asked me, and I eyed him.

"How do you know my name?"

"I know a lot of things, sweetheart. I'm a man of many resources."

"What if I don't want you to have my number?"

"I'll find you one way or another. It's your choice."

"You're a stalker or something?' I asked him, and he laughed.

"No, not at all, beautiful. I just like what I see. And when I want something, I go after it."

"You know my name, but I don't know yours?"

"It's Jamie, but the streets call me Terror," he said.

My eyes sort of bucked. Mr. Terror himself in the flesh. So, this was who they were talking about.

"Okay, so what would you like for me to call you?" I asked him.

I wanted to know more like why was my brother working for him?

"You can call me anything you want," and then he leaned in closer to whisper in my ear.

"I would prefer daddy," he said, and I looked at him.

He smirked, and I shook my head. This man had a lot of balls. Daddy? Shit, I only had one daddy, and he wasn't here anymore.

"No, I would prefer not. But it was nice meeting you, Jamie," I stated and was about to walk away from him.

"You walking away too soon. So, what about that number? Is it okay if I call you sometime?" he asked, and I pondered it for a minute. I didn't have much to say to him, or any man, for that matter.

"No, I'm okay." I smiled, and he frowned a little.

I mean, it wasn't a lot, but that small inkling let me know he was used to having his way with women and everything else.

"Well, how about this? You take my number and call whenever you feel up to it. I would love to show you a good time and how a woman is supposed to be treated by a real man," he said.

"Yeah, maybe I can do that." I smiled and pulled out my phone.

He rattled his number off to me and I punched it in my phone. Once that was done, he kissed the back of my hand again and told me I wouldn't regret calling him. I didn't know what it was about him, but I liked his swag. An older man and all, he was swagged out.

"Have a great day, beautiful, and don't forget to use that number. And, again, I'm sorry for your loss. Kade was a good kid," he expressed and walked away.

I looked behind me and felt someone's eyes on me. Kade's girlfriend, Nisa, was staring at me with a blank expression on her face, and I wondered what was up with her.

I shrugged it off and went looking for Knox and the rest of the crew. I wondered why he didn't come when I called out his name, and now I knew why. He was in the basement of the hall getting high with Prince and their friends Benz and Tony.

"Knox, really? You can't get fucking high in these people's shit," I snapped at him, and they all looked at me.

"Man, twin, I'll pay for whatever they gonna charge, but I ain't going outside smoking shit," he snapped back.

"Knox, we have guests upstairs. Couldn't this wait?" I argued.

"Nah, it couldn't."

He was nonchalant, and I knew he felt guilty because of Kade's death, but I kept telling him over and over again that he had nothing to do with Kade's death, and he shouldn't place the blame on himself.

"Whatever, Knox. You gonna pay for it too," I sassed and walked back up the stairs.

Before I could reenter the hall, I leaned against the wall and exhaled deeply. I was too young to always feel like I was stressing, but I was. I touched the left side of my chest and rubbed it in an up and down motion. It always felt like my chest was tight; as if I was about to have a heart attack or something. I breathed in and out about six more times before I gathered myself and walked back into the hall.

As soon as I tried to head for my seat, here comes Nisa. She stopped me mid-way.

"What's wrong?" I eyed her.

"I need to talk to you."

"Right now?"

"Yes."

"About what?"

Nisa and I had already talked. I didn't think it was anything more that she had to say about Kade to me.

"Terror…" she said, and that piqued my interest.

"Okay," I replied as she led me out the hall and to the steps of the hall.

I sat ready to listen, and I was all ears.

YOUNG NIGGAS AND LOVE

KNOX

"Look, man, Ion give a fuck whatchu talking about, you got a whole nigga who done came in yo shit while we fucking. Then you threatened to call the police on me when I took yo car and shit. You foul as shit for that, ma," I told Gianna's stupid ass.

She was on the other end of my phone going off. Talking about how she was there for me when none else was and how I only used her for what I wanted.

"I'm saying, Knox, you didn't even give me a chance to explain," she said.

"What's to explain, man? That nigga came inside yo shit! Now what if he had a banger on him? I woulda just been a dead nigga then."

"Jake isn't like that, and he misunderstood our situation. Come on, baby, you know I wouldn't do you like that. I'm the one who was there for you when you were locked down. Now look, you on some other shit with me. I apologized over and over, Knox."

"I'm just tryna figure out why Benz even gave yo ass my number."

"Knox, don't be like that."

"I'm serious, man. Ion need them types of problems. I don't wanna have to dead a nigga over yo ass."

"I'm serious too! Knox, come on now. Let me come over and make it up to you," she said.

I thought on it for a minute. I hadn't touched a bitch since Kade's funeral. It was still fucking me up in the head how my lil brother ended up dead. I was determined to get answers.

"Look, man, come through and leave the drama at yo fucking crib," I spat at her ditzy ass.

She agreed, and I hung up the phone.

I looked around my new crib, and I couldn't do anything but smile to myself. My pops got me and my sister right. I had two mill in my bank account, and a small house on the southside of Chicago, 'cause at the end of the day, I was still a hood nigga. I couldn't live with the uppity folks; that shit wasn't in my blood. And I had a whip. I finally got my state ID. and my driver's license, so a nigga was good to go.

All I was thinking about was never going back broke again in my life. I wanted to flip my shit, and ASAP. Prince was telling me about his homie, Javier Billions, who was the biggest connect in the Midwest. Besides Prince's brother, Terror, there were no other niggas running the southside. Prince and Benz were tryna do a lil something, but that's about it. I figure I can get in where I fit in. In the drug world, there was always money to be made, and it was always a muthafucka out there willing to sell the shit.

My cell vibrated on my coffee table, and I picked it up. It was Spirit texting me, and a smile came to my face. I had been meaning to hit her up, but with so much shit going on, especially the situation with Kade, I didn't have time to.

Spirit: Hey You!

Me: What's up sexy ass

Spirit: Lol! Nothing much, just tryna see if you're busy

Me: I'm caught up doing a lil something right now, but what's up? You good?

Spirit: I'm good, call or text me when you're free. I'm about to head to work in a lil while

Me: I got you! And you about to stop working at the fucking club shawty!

Spirit: Whatever, Knox! Lmao

I didn't know why she thought that shit was a joke because in no way was I joking or playing about that shit. I didn't wanna fuck with a chick that every nigga in the hood has seen her goodies. Fuck that. The shit wasn't cool. I wondered how Spirit got to that fucking point. I didn't expect her to be some fucking stripper. She was the type of chick where education was always her first priority. I understood life happened, but damn, it must've gotten really bad for her.

My thoughts then roamed to Kimora. Twin was mad at me for how I was acting at the funeral, and I meant to apologize to her. It was wrong for me to take my frustrations out on her when she didn't do shit to me. I was simply confused, heartbroken, and angry about my lil brother I needed fucking answers about his death, and I wasn't gonna stop until I got them. He wasn't killed at the club that night. They found his body in an alley. That shit was fucked up how they did him dirty.

My doorbell rang, and I got off my couch and walked to it, I opened the door, and standing on the other side was Gianna. Her thick ass was standing there looking sexy as hell. She wore a grin on her face that I shoulda knocked the fuck off.

"What's good, man?" I asked her.

"Hey, bae," she chimed as I stepped to the side and allowed her in.

I smacked her ass as hard as I could as she passed me.

"Owww!" she yelped, and I chuckled.

"Why would you do that, asshole?" she said, facing me.

"Man, that's what the fuck you get. Have some big, fat ass, musty looking ass nigga come back through yo shit again, and we gonna have some muthafucking problems," I said, getting in her face, and she smirked.

"Are you jealous?"

"You wish. I'm cautious, baby. There's a difference," I spat.

"Whatever, Knox. I told you it was a mistake. Now do you forgive me or what?" She eyed me.

"Nah, I don't."

"What can I do to make it up to you?" she asked in a sultry voice.

"Get on yo knees and suck my dick," I whispered.

"That's all, baby?"

"I want more, but I'll tell you when. For now, I wanna see yo pretty ass lips on my dick, and take yo time. I want you to make love to this muthafucka," I said in a husky tone, and she dropped to her knees.

She pulled my dick out of my basketball shorts and inserted my nigga in her warm mouth. I closed my eyes and gripped the back of her head. Made her ass suck my shit until I came down her throat. I wanted to punish Gianna's ass in the worst way for that sneaky shit. I hated a sneaky bitch.

"So, tell me what you want from me, Knox Eldredge," Spirit asked as we sat in the park by her house.

I thought of some corny shit. Some shit only females would dig. I decided to make us a lunch and have a picnic in the park while talking.

Since I was kicking it with Gianna three days ago, I couldn't get up with Spirit like I wanted to, but today, we finally made time for each other. I was glad because I wanted to see her ass in the worst way.

"I don't want shit from you but to be yo man. that's it. I wanna take care of you, fuck you right, make some babies with you, and all that good shit." I smirked, and she looked at me with shock written over her face.

"Wait a minute, Knox. What happened to the part about dating first?"

"Man, has anyone ever told you that you look like JuJu, Cameron's girlfriend?" I told her, ignoring her question.

"Yeah, I get that a lot. But, again, what the fuck happened to dating, like I said before?"

"What we gotta date for, Spirit? I know yo ass already. I've been wanting you for years, and over time, you tried to play a nigga. But, I'm still the same nigga, and I still want yo ass," I told her.

She looked at me and smiled.

"Knox, I don't think you want me. I come with a lot of shit, honestly. Let me ask you this. What do you want in a woman? What's your ideal woman? Because I might not be it."

"I don't have an ideal woman. Be who you are, but don't be sneaky 'cause I hate sneaky bitches. I can't stand liars, and dishonor is a no, no. In fact, all that shit goes together," I told her, and she nodded.

"Whatchu want in a man?"

"I want him to be all mine. No matter what. I don't want a man who is gonna step out on his girl when shit gets rough. I don't want a man who's going to leave when shit gets rough, because I've learned that life is rough, and only the strong survive out here. I need someone who is willing to survive with me," she said.

"I can fuck with that," I replied, and she burst into laughter.

"You can fuck with that, huh?"

"Yeah... I mean, I ain't the perfect nigga, but I'm something close to it."

"I just bet you are."

"So, who is that clown I knocked out that night?"

"My ex-boyfriend," she replied with a roll of her eyes.

"He's a goofy because I woulda never let you break up with me. Shit, once we together, we together. Ain't no breaking up, bihhhhh," I said, and she laughed again.

"Wait… Did you just call me a bitch?"

"Shawty, shut that shit up. You gonna be my bitch. That's what you are. Some chicks get upset by the saying, but my meaning of the statement and other muthafuckas meaning of it is totally different. When I say you my bitch, that means you're my everything. You wanna fight the feeling right now, Spirit, and I'm gonna allow you to continue to do you, but know this; You gon' be mine and you know it, or you wouldn't be out here with a nigga," I told her, and she just stared at me but she didn't say a word

"Fuck you looking at, man? Kiss me already," I told her, and she smiled as she leaned down and softly pecked my lips.

"Just like I thought. Them bitches soft as fuck." I grinned.

Me and Spirit sat in the park until the sun was going down, and she told me she had to leave to go home and check on her mother. I kissed her one last time and hopped in my ride as she hopped in her car. I watched as she sped off, heading back to her house.

Once she was gone I headed for the crib. I pulled my phone out of my glove compartment and I had ten missed calls from Gianna's bug a boo ass.

THIS WAS NEVER PART OF
THE PLAN

KIMORA

My peep toe high heels clacked against the pavement of the parking lot. My nerves were rattled, and I swear I brushed my hair with my hands over a thousand times. I had never been to this restaurant, and my nerves were all over the place.

Once I got to the entrance of the restaurant, I went inside, and my eyes scanned around. There seated in the corner of the restaurant tucked to the side was Jamie aka Terror. I finally took him up on his offer to take me out on a date. I wanted to see what he was about.

I walked to the hostess and told her who I was there to see. She led me to where he was seated, and when I got to the table, I noticed the two men standing guard behind him. It was crazy that he was the only person in the restaurant with bodyguards.

"How are you, beautiful?" he asked me.

"I'm good." I smiled at him as he got out his seat and pulled my chair out for me.

'Thank You."

"Anything for a beautiful woman such like yourself," he replied as he took his seat.

I stared at him, and I shouldn't have. He was wearing a nice suit with the shoes to match. It was charcoal grey, and the cologne he sported smelled so damn good.

I picked up a menu and looked it over but he grabbed it out of my hands.

"No need to look at that. I ordered for you already," he said.

I smiled but I was confused. "Oh, you did? You don't even know what I like?"

"It doesn't matter. What matters is you being lady like. All you need is a garden salad, no dressing because its fattening, a glass of sparkling water, and a chicken breast thinly sliced," he announced, and I chuckled.

This man had to be something crazy if he through he was gonna come at me like that.

"You know what, Terror? Thanks, but no thanks for the date. I don't like the fact that you're insulting my weight. Telling me what to eat? No, that's not gonna happen," I spat.

I was about to get up until his voice boomed out.

"Sit down," he said in a deep voice, and I looked at him. "I said, sit down, Kimora," he said a little bit softer.

For some reason, I obliged.

"I'm telling you what you should eat for your health, not

because of your weight. If I had a problem with your weight, I would have never approached you."

"But you ain't my daddy. And I like to eat, as you can see," I sassed. Even though I had cut down on the things I ate, I still didn't like the fact that he was telling me what to do or what to eat.

"Look, let's start over. I'm usually in charge of everything, and I apologize. I don't wanna come off a certain way toward you. Okay?" He extended his hand, and I just looked at it.

"You're kind of rude, but okay, let's start over," I said as I took his hand into mine and shook it.

"I know. I get that a lot. I'm Jamie, and it's nice to meet you." He smiled.

"Kimora," I replied, playing his little game.

"You can get whatever you wanna get off the menu, and I will never speak out of line again to you," he said, and I nodded.

Once the waitress came, I ordered my food and a glass of red wine. I wasn't really a drinker, but drinking with Jessica help me get used to it. Red wine was it for me, though. Anything outside of that, I wasn't drinking.

"So, tell me. Do you have any kids?'

"No."

"And, why not?" I asked him.

I was curious because he was so much older than me. I just knew he some children roaming around here.

"Because being a made man means no children allowed. The type of lifestyle I live, it wasn't meant for me to have anyone I care about in this world," he said, and I only nodded my head because I fully understood.

"Oh, I understand."

"Do you really?"

"I do."

"Tell me about you, Kimora."

"What is it to tell?"

"Tell me everything. Your dreams, your fears, your goals. What makes you angry, what makes you sad," he said, and I didn't feel comfortable enough to tell him anything about me or my life.

"Let's just say I had it rough growing up. Some things I would rather not talk about. Some things I wish I didn't remember because my soul is still scarred."

"We all have scars. How you choose to heal is what matters," he said and winked at me.

By the end of the night, I was intrigued by Mr. Terror. For him to be terrorizing the streets, he didn't come off like that toward me. I went back home all smiles. Dinner was great, and I hadn't felt this special in a long time.

"KIMORA! MORA!" I HEARD MY NAME BEING CALLED WHILE I was still half asleep.

When I looked up, Jessica was standing in my bedroom. She had a shocked expression on her face, and I hopped up because lately, my life hasn't been going right.

"What happened?" I immediately asked.

"Nothing happened. You have to see this," she said, and I

got out of bed and followed her out of my bedroom. We went downstairs, and when we got in the living room, there were at least fifty shopping bags from different stores in the living room.

"What the hell is this?" I asked confused.

"They're for you," she said with a smile on her face.

"For who? For me?" I asked.

"Yes, for you. Whoever Jamie is sent them this morning. The gifts haven't stopped coming."

"Wait... you gotta be playing," I said as a smile overtook my face.

"Girl, whoever this Jamie person is has got to be feeling you," she squealed, and I went around the living room grabbing the bags and going through them.

I pulled out designer dresses, jewelry, and shoes. I didn't know how this man knew my size—clothes and shoes—but he was right on the money.

"Oh my God," I whispered as I looked everything over.

Since I'd gotten my father's money, I hadn't done anything for myself. I lived my life privately, and I didn't buy unnecessary bullshit. The only expensive thing I owned was my car. And even that wasn't that much money. So, this small gesture flattered me.

"Sooooo who is he?" Jessica asked.

"It's just a dude I met."

"Well, this dude looks like he has a lot of money, and it doesn't look like legal money. In my line of work, I've seen quite a few drug dealers get thrown into jail for life, and even their girlfriends sometimes had to do some time."

"But, I'm not his girlfriend. He's just a friend, Jessica," I reassured her

"I'm not saying you are. I'm only saying, be careful, Mora," she said with the lawyer in her seeping out.

I nodded, and Jessica kissed me on the cheek then walked away.

I went to my bedroom and grabbed my cell phone off my bed. I dialed up Terror, and he answered on the first ring.

"You like your gifts?" he asked.

"I do. I do. Thank You. But you know you didn't have to do that for me."

"You don't have to tell me what I didn't have to do. I know it already. You deserve nothing but the best," he said, making me blush.

"Well, thank you, Terror."

"No problem, beautiful. But look, let me call you back in a minute I'm out handling some business. I have reservations set up for us tonight at Mistro's steak house. It's at 7:30, so don't be late, Kimora," he spat and hung up the phone.

I looked at the phone, and I was confused. Did he just hang up on me? Did he just demand we have dinner together? How the hell did he even know where I lived? As all those questions ran through my mind, my phone beeped with a text message from him.

Jamie/Terror: Wear the light blue dress in the Gucci bag tonight for dinner.

Me: Okay

Jamie/Terror: And make sure you don't wear any panties underneath it.

I ignored his last text message because he had me

twisted. I was still technically a virgin since I hadn't had sex with anyone in my life willingly. Trey was a different story because he raped me. I didn't ask for him to take my virginity, but he did, and I will always be haunted by that shit he pulled.

I left my bedroom and went to grab all those shopping bags. As I took them back to my room, I felt like pretty woman. Terror was showing out, and I didn't know how I was supposed to take it.

I called up Nisa, and she answered on the first ring. I didn't have friends, and Nisa seemed pretty cool. Ever since Kade's death, she'ds been calling and texting me. I could tell she didn't have a lot of people in her life either.

"Hey, Kimora."

"Hey, Nisa. How you doing?" I asked her.

"I'm good." She exhaled.

"I was just calling to check on you and to see how you're holding up."

"I'm fine, how you doing?"

"I'm good. I went out with Terror last night."

"Oh, you did?" she asked, seeming surprised.

"I did. And he's everything you've said he would be."

"So, how do you wanna move with this? Because, honestly, Kimora, I believed Kade with everything he told me about Terror," she said.

"I'm gonna handle it. You just make sure you don't say anything to Knox. You promised me."

"I know, and I won't. I just want you to be careful because… because Terror is fucking dangerous."

"I know," I replied as I smirked, thinking about my plan.

As of today, I wasn't afraid of danger. In fact, I welcomed it. I've become a new woman for several reasons, and a lot of muthafuckas were gonna pay for all the bullshit they caused in my life

I'M A SELF-MADE NIGGA

PRINCE

"Where you going, daddy?" Dana asked me as I put my shirt on.

I had moves to make, and I couldn't sit around and not do shit but lay up. That wasn't in me. I mean the freak in her ass was all good, but pussy didn't pay bills nor put food on the table. I had a meeting today with my connect.

"I got moves to make, ma," I told her nosy ass.

That's all she needed to know at the moment.

"Oh, okay. Are you coming back tonight? Do you want me to stay up for you?" she inquired, and I only looked at her.

"Nah, I might not come back this way. But keep that shit tight." I eyed her ass.

She smiled as I placed my J's on my feet. I grabbed my

cell phone and car keys and kissed the top of her forehead then was out the door. I hopped in my ride and sped toward Ruth's Chris downtown on Michigan avenue.

These niggas said it was important, so I knew when they called it was only right to come. I wouldn't disrespect them and say fuck them in any way. I admired the way the Billions brothers put in work. How they demanded their respect. I wasn't dick riding or no shit like that, but I called it like I saw it.

When I pulled up to the restaurant, I valet parked my whip and went inside. Once I told the hostess who I was there to see, I was led to the table in the back for private meetings and shit like that. When I got to the back, all three brothers, their wives, and my fucking brother, Terror, and Kimora were there. My eyes bucked when I saw her. First off, I was fucking confused when I saw him with her. What the fuck was she doing with Terror's crazy ass, and did Knox know she was with him?

"Good evening, gentlemen." I smirked as I took my seat at the table.

"Fuck nigga, fuck took you so long?" Jax Billions grimaced as he looked at me.

"I was tied up with some shit, big homie, my bad." I apologized for being late.

"Aight, man, that shit gonna be ya last time being late. We don't operate like that," he spat back, and I only nodded my head.

"So, what's good, y'all? What's this all about?" I questioned as I looked around the table.

"Ladies, could you excuse us please?" Javier Billions

spoke to the women, and they excused themselves from the table.

I glanced over at my big brother and exhaled deeply. Shit starting ass nigga right here.

"We heard you was stepping on some toes, my nigga. And I don't do business like this. But after doing some research, I see that you and this nigga Terror are brothers. I called this meeting because we need to hash out some differences, so money can continuously be made," Javier spoke.

"All I gotta ask is how I'm stepping on his toes? I don't get it?" I asked.

I wasn't serving in Terror's territory; I was doing my own thang.

"Because, muthafucka, I didn't have competition! And now you're the fucking competition! My own fucking blood," Terror barked, and I chuckled.

"Nigga, you got yo own set, and I'm nowhere near where yo people be at, man. Get the fuck on with all that shit." I snapped.

"Yo, you muthafuckas gotta get this shit in order. We don't need any bad blood on the streets. It's enough room for all you muthafuckas to make some fucking money," Jax snapped at us, and I didn't say anything.

"What's the solution gonna be? Are you gonna respect each other's turf, or do you niggas wanna go to war? War makes us lose money, so think fucking wisely before you answer," Javier added.

"Nah, I'm good. I was never in this nigga's way. He's just mad I'm not tryna work for him. Shit, I'm my own man. I don't need a muthafucka to put me on. I put myself on," I snapped, staring Terror in his eyes.

I wanted this bitch ass nigga to feel where the fuck I was coming from.

"Well, he's good. Are you good?" Juelz Billions asked Terror, and he smirked, staring at me.

"Yeah, I'm good," he replied.

"Well, I'm glad that shit is over. Now go and get my fucking wife and tell her to come and eat," Jax said to the waitress who was posted in the corner.

She scurried off and did as she was told, and I got out of my seat. I had a feeling that this wasn't gonna be over any time soon. Terror only agreed because he didn't wanna face the backlash from the Billions. I knew it was a war coming between me and my brother because Terror was used to having his way, and by me not giving in to his demands, the only thing he saw from it was blood.

As I walked away from the table, Kimora walked past me. I grabbed her by her elbow and walked her backward toward the entrance. We went outside, and she stared me up and down with a mug on her face. When I say she was fucking beautiful, that word was an understatement. Her full face had make up on it, something I've never seen before, and her long hair was brushed up tightly into a ponytail, which hung down her back. The rocks in her ears were glistening, and the blue, tight fitted dress that hugged her thick ass curves had my mouth watering. Kimora didn't look like the same person.

"Why you grabbing on me like that, Prince?" she asked.

"Why you in this bitch with Terror? That ain't a good look for you, Ma," I told her, and she exhaled.

"Because I'm grown, Prince, and I can do what I want," she sassed, and I chuckled.

I never knew Kimora had so much fucking confidence. This was something new on her, but I liked it.

"Do you know what type of man my brother is? You don't know the half. You don't know what the fuck you getting yourself into. I wonder does Knox know you're here?" I questioned.

"Knox isn't my father, and neither are you. Terror is a good dude, and he treats me nice. That's the only reason I'm out on a date with him right now. And, again, I'm grown, Prince," she snapped.

"Yeah… you right. You are grown, but that's some dumb ass shit to be getting smart at the mouth when I'm telling you for your own good, don't fuck with the nigga. He's my brother, and I'm telling you what I know."

"Wait… he's your brother?"

"Yeah… you didn't just hear me when I said that shit?" I laughed at her.

"Nah, I didn't hear you." She smiled at me.

I was about to respond until the doors of the restaurant opened and Terror walked out. He had a grimace on his face as the valet pulled up with his car.

"Jamie…" Kimora tried to say, but he held his hand up at her and stopped her in her tracks.

"Save it," he spat and hopped in his ride.

He peeled away from the restaurant, and she stood there

stuck, not knowing what to say. This nigga straight fucking left her.

"Oh my God, this nigga just left me," she squealed, and I chuckled.

"What the hell is funny? You find this shit funny?" she spewed at me.

"I told… I told yo ass that nigga wasn't right, but you weren't tryna hear what I'm saying."

"Fuck you!" she scoffed, and I laughed loudly.

"Don't be mad at me, the fuck nigga probably mad you was out here talking with me."

"Fuck him."

"You need a ride or something?" I asked her, still chuckling.

"Yeah," she gave in, and I motioned for the valet to go and get my car.

When they pulled my car around, I opened the front door for her, and she slid inside. On the drive back, we both were quiet.

"Do you even know where you taking me?" she asked.

"Yeah, to the crib with ole girl, right?" I glanced over at her.

"Nah, take me to your brother's house. My car is parked there."

My nostrils instantly flared.

"I'm not taking you to that nigga's crib, man. You better Uber yo ass over there."

She mugged me.

"I'm serious, man."

"Then let me out, nigga. You and ya brother some sort of fucked up around here."

"And you not? Fucking with Terror's old ass. You gotta be tripping"

"Prince, I'm not about to go back and forth with you about my business. It seems like you're jealous of your own brother, if you ask me."

"I ain't jealous of that bitch ass nigga. He ain't got shit I want," I spewed angrily. She had just pissed me off with that goofy ass shit she said out of her mouth.

"Whatever. Say what you want, but that's how it seems to me."

"I'm telling Knox on yo ass, man."

She waved me off, and I chuckled.

"So, tell me, Prince, whatchu doing with yo self in these streets. I never took you for a drug dealer."

"I'm tryna survive, ya know."

"You coulda went back to school, ya know."

"And why you ain't back in school?" I eyed her, and she shrugged.

"It's not for me. I'm not a people person, as you can see."

"You are, you just don't know it yet. You're a dope soul. I just wish you realized it."

"Did you realize it when we were in high school? You were just like the rest of these muthafuckas. You looked over me as well," she snapped.

I looked at her and then back at the road.

"That shit ain't true, Kimora. I definitely saw it, but you didn't see yourself. You were too busy being scared of the world and never having a backbone or defending yourself. You expected Knox to be your everything, and he couldn't be," I told her ass, but she glared at me with tears in her eyes.

"Let me out, muthafucka!" she screamed, and I ignored her.

The truth hurts.

"I said, let me the fuck out!" she screamed again, and still, I kept driving.

She wanted to go into a rage when I was only telling her the real. The next thing I knew, this crazy muthafucka opened my car door while it was still moving. I hurriedly pulled over on the side street and turned my car off. She hopped out and started walking down the street with her arms folded across her chest.

"Aye yo!" I called out, running to catch up with her.

"What!" she screamed at me.

"Aye, man, what's good with that shit? Why would you open the door to a moving fucking car?" I snapped.

"You got me fucked up! You didn't want me in high school! No one did! And if you expect me to take what the fuck you saying to me without lashing out, then you're wrong! I know what I was! I was the one who lived it! I was the one who dealt with every fucked up thing that was handed to me! You sitting here talking about my fucking self-esteem! Talking about a fucking backbone? I don't need no muthafucking reminders! But today, I'm a new woman, and I'm not taking anybody's shit! And I mean NOBODY," she screamed at me as tears fell from her eyes

I felt bad as fuck for what I said to her. I definitely didn't mean to come off that way. Seeing her cry broke my heart. I walked up to her and pulled her in my arms. She tried to fight me off, but I wouldn't let her.

"I'm sorry, Kimora. I'm sorry," I whispered as I hugged her tight.

She cried in my chest, and I felt like shit. She calmed down some and then took a step back from me.

"It's all good, Prince. I'm better than I've ever been, and it's cool. But sometimes when you're reminded of your past, it hurts," she said.

I didn't respond. Instead, I leaned in and kissed her juicy lips, something I've been wanting to do since she had been with me.

"Wait... what you doing?" she asked, and I brought her closer to me.

"Something I've been wanting to do all fucking night," I whispered as I kissed her again, this time adding a lil tongue into the mix.

She wrapped her arms around me and kissed me back. We were standing in the middle of an unknown street kissing like our lives depended on it. I had to pull myself away because my dick was getting hard.

"Damn, that was nice," she said in a low tone as she blushed, and I smirked.

"Aye, let me take you to dinner?" I asked, looking in her eyes.

"I don't know. I'm dealing with Terror right now," she said, and that only pissed me off.

"I shouldn't have even kissed you, Prince. That's wrong of us"

"Aight, man, whatever you say. How about this? Let's go

to dinner as friends. We need to catch up anyway." I grinned, and she eyed me.

"Okay, I guess we can go to dinner as friends only. And no more kissing on me," she sassed.

I chuckled as I grabbed her hand and led her back to my car. We got inside, and we pulled off. I took her to get her car from in front of Terror's crib, and once I saw that she was inside and okay, I drove off with thoughts of her juicy ass lips on my mind.

WHEN IT'S ALL SAID AND DONE

SPIRIT

"**K**nox, why are you doing this?" I asked him as we strolled through River Oaks mall.

He was buying me everything my eyes feasted upon, and I was confused as to where he got all this fucking money from since he had just gotten out of jail.

"I do what I do, shawty. You know that." He smirked at me, and I swear the way he looked at me made me cream my panties every time.

"Well, I thank you so much. I love everything I got tonight."

"No problem, bae. Shit, I'm working on getting the pussy." He laughed, and I pushed him.

"Stop playing. Who's to say you gon' get some of this pretty kitty?" I teased, but I was dying to fuck him in the worst way. I just had to maintain my image. It wouldn't be right to just bust it open for him.

"Shit, I say. I'm gon' get the pussy, you know I am, so stop playing with me, shawty."

"Whatever, Knox." I laughed him off.

Me and Knox had been kicking it since the picnic we had that day, and I was feeling him heavy. He showered me with so much attention, and I swear I would think I'm dreaming if I didn't know any better. He was gangsta, yet so fucking gentle. Everything I wanted in a man.

After shopping for a while, we left the mall and headed for his house. We were gonna kick it for a while until it was time for me to relieve the nurse who took care of my mom. We stopped at Chipotle, and I got a steak and chicken bowl and a Pepsi.

Once we made it to his crib, we went inside, and I plopped down on his bed, ready to get my grub on. I was fucking starving.

"Whatchu wanna watch?" he asked me.

"I don't care. You got a Firestick or cable?"

"Both." He smirked, and I shook my head.

Knox was as cocky as they came, and he always had some smart-ass comeback out of his damn mouth.

"Let's watch *Girl's Trip*," I suggested, and he frowned.

"Man, what?"

"I said—"

"I know whatchu said, but I was just making sure I heard you right. Hell nawl, man. You better think of something else," he snapped.

"Alright, let's watch Black Panther then."

"Aight, now that's something we can watch." He smiled proudly, and I laughed.

Knox put the movie on, and I started to eat my food. After eating, I curled up under him, and he gently rubbed my back. He smelled so good, and I could lay up under him all day.

"You ready to give me some of that pretty kitty?" he asked, making me burst into laughter.

"Boy, what? You are a mess, Knox!" I squealed, pulling myself away from him, but he grabbed me back by the back of neck and brought my lips close to his.

He kissed me lightly, biting my bottom lip, and I moaned a little. Damn, this nigga was such a turn on.

"Dance for me," he said in a husky tone, and I eyed him.

"What?"

"I said, dance for me. I wanna see you shake that ass just for me," he said casually, and I smiled.

I was low key ashamed that he asked me to dance for him but at the same time enticed by it.

I got off the bed and stood in front of him. He stared at me with those big, pretty, light brown eyes, and I fell in love just by looking at him. It felt like he was staring into my soul.

"I need some music," I replied, and he nodded as he grabbed the remote control to his television. He had a smart TV, so iHeart radio was already programmed in it.

The music came on, and I had to laugh at what played.

"Trap, Trap money benny, aye she got me in my feelings. Kek,e do you love me? Are you riding? Said you'll never ever leave from beside me, 'cause I want ya, and I need ya."

I burst into laughter.

"I am not dancing to this!" I squealed.

"Aight, man, I quit. Come here," he said, and I walked between his legs.

He grabbed me by my hips and pulled me closer to him.

"Spirit, do you love me, said I want ya…" He looked in my eyes, and I smiled.

"Knox, you're milking it," I said as he chuckled.

"Nah, straight up though, shawty. What's good, baby? You riding or what?"

"What we doing, Knox?" I wanted to know.

Shit, I was still having issues with Tyree's ass that I needed to work out.

"We can do whatever you wanna do, beautiful. All I need to know is if you riding for me. I wanna fuck with you the long way, Spirit. I know this seems like it's a spur of the moment type of thing, but I've always wanted you. I feel like this is my chance to show you the type of nigga I really am," he said, and I couldn't do anything but kiss his lips.

I had never heard words like that from a man, but I didn't know if this was what I wanted moving forward because I was still confused.

Knox kissed me with so much passion. He slowly ran his hands up and down my back. I pulled away and dropped between his legs on my knees. He stared at me as I undid his pants. I pulled out his dick, and just looking at it, my kitty kat starting purring. His dick was long, thick, and full of veins. I licked my lips before I placed him in my mouth. The minute I sucked on the head of his dick, he let out a moan of ecstasy.

"Damn, shawty, just like that." He groaned, and I put my all into it.

I sucked the head of his dick, flicking my tongue back and forth on it, and then I played with his balls, which really drove him wild.

"Man, fuck all that. Stand that ass up," he demanded, pulling his dick out of my mouth.

I looked up at him in shock, but he eyed me as if to say, *do what the fuck I say and right now,* so I complied and did as he asked. I stood up and stripped out of my clothing.

Knox picked me up and tossed me onto his bed. He placed my leg above his shoulder and dived head first into my pussy.

"Ahhhhhh Shitttt," I hissed the moment I felt his tongue connect with my clit.

I gripped the back of his head as my eyes rolled. He was sucking and playing with my pussy for dear life.

"Ahhhhhh… Ohhhhhhh shit, baby," I screamed as I felt my nut coming on strong.

Before I could warn him, I busted all over his face.

"Yesssssss, daddy. Mmmhmmm yesssssss," I cried.

"You like that shit, don't you?" he asked with a smirk etched on his face.

I didn't say anything. I breathed in and out, trying to catch my breath. I didn't even wanna fuck no more. I wanted to crawl up in bed and suck my thumb after receiving head like that.

"I do. Baby… I do." I exhaled deeply.

"Come here," his husky voice demanded as he got up and lay on his back.

I walked over to him, and he motioned for me to sit down on his dick. I eased down on him, slowly inserting him in my pussy. When he filled me up, I had to catch my breath for a minute.

I slowly grinded my hips until I caught a good rhythm. The dick was feeling so good I had to close my eyes to relish the moment.

"Ahhhh shit, shawty, ride this mufucka," he whispered, staring up at me while biting his bottom lip.

That drove me crazy, and I started throwing this ass, bucking back against him as he held on to my hips for the ride.

"Mmmhmmm, daddy," I moaned as he leaned up and placed one of my titties in his mouth.

He was sucking my titties while I was riding him, and he was smacking my ass with one hand. The feeling was sensational.

"Uhhhh, KNOXXXXXXXXXXXX, baby. I'm about to cummmmm," I cried as the feeling overtook me.

He gripped my ass cheeks and thrust himself upward, feeding me his full dick in long strokes, and that shit had me over the top. I came so hard that my body started shaking uncontrollably, I thought he didn't cum until I felt his dick get extra hard, and then it went flaccid. I rolled off of him, trying to catch my breath.

"Damn, pretty kitty got a nigga right," he hissed, and I laughed

"Shut up!" I squealed as I leaned over and gently kissed his lips.

He cuddled me as I fell asleep lying on his chest. This

was somewhere I wanted to be. It felt good being right there with him.

THE SOUND OF SOMEONE BEATING ON KNOX'S FRONT DOOR woke both of us out of our slumber. Knox got out of the bed asshole naked and grabbed his gun from underneath his mattress. My eyes bucked at the sight of the gun.

"What's... what's going on?'

"Chill... it's all good," he threw over his shoulder as he walked out of the bedroom, still with no clothes on.

I was nervous as fuck. I wasn't used to this type of shit. I got off the bed and threw on Knox's t-shirt that was lying on the floor. I tiptoed out of the bedroom and walked into the living room. Knox was standing in the doorway butt ass naked with the gun at his side arguing with some chick. She looked past him and spotted me.

"Who the fuck is that? Is that why you're in here without any clothes on? You in here fucking?" she screamed loud as fuck, and I was truly embarrassed.

I looked at the clock on the wall, and it was midnight. I was supposed to have been home to be with my mother. I chuckled at her and walked off from them. Once I got back in the bedroom, I placed my clothes on my body.

I grabbed my shit and walked back to the front. Knox looked at me completely surprised when he saw that I was fully dressed. Shaking my head, I walked to my car. What I didn't have time for was a bitch and her antics. I didn't have a man anymore, and this was one of the reasons why. I also hated the fact that Knox lied to me. He didn't tell me he was dealing with somebody.

I hopped in my ride and peeled away from Knox's crib. My mind was spinning while I was driving. All I could think about was I how I gave my body to him, and now this fucking drama. If I wanted drama, I could've stayed with Tyree's ass.

My cell started to ring. I looked down and saw that it was Knox calling me. I let out a deep sigh, but I didn't answer. I didn't wanna hear any of the lies or excuses. He could save it. My phone rang over and over until I got frustrated.

"What!" I screamed into the phone.

"Damn, it's like that? I was just calling to check up on you," Tyree's voice boomed, and I softened mine a little bit.

"Oh, hey. I'm a little frustrated right now, but what's up?" I asked him.

"Shit much, I just called to say. I... I miss you, Spirit. I know I've been acting a fool, but—"

I stopped him in his tracks before he could continue.

"Just come over," I told him, and he agreed.

I hung up my phone and went into my home. I hopped in the shower to wash the scent of Knox off me. As I showered, tears fell from my eyes. The minute I started to get attached, it was always something pulling me back.

A WOMAN ON A MISSION

KIMORA

"So, damn, shawty. Tell me why you ain't never tried to fuck with a nigga?" Prince asked me as we sat at the Italian restaurant near Jessica's house.

I didn't have to explain that to him because he knew the reason why. Prince had asked me out on a date after he dropped me off at my car that night, and I accepted. Now here we are.

"You know why, Prince." I chuckled as I slid some pasta in my mouth.

"Yeah, whatever, man. That self-esteem shit ain't got nothing to do with it," he claimed.

"I like you, though, Mora, and a lot."

I blushed when he said that. He had been coming on strong ever since that night at the restaurant, but I still had a bigger picture to achieve with this nigga Jamie.

I've had Nisa look into some things for me, and slowly but surely, everything was falling into place. My mind zoned out for a minute as I thought about Jamie.

"Aye, shawty, fuck wrong with you?' Prince said, breaking my train of thought.

I looked up at him and smiled.

"I'm sorry. My mind just got lost in a trance."

"Well, I hope you ain't thinking about my brother." He raised an eyebrow, and I rolled my eyes.

"Nah, I'm not."

"Why the fuck you fucking with the old nigga anyway?" he asked me, and I shrugged.

"Why are we talking about him? I thought we were on a date or whatever this is."

"We are, I'm just asking questions."

"Well, don't ask those questions. Now what are some other things you would like to know?" I asked, switching the subject.

I wasn't in the mood for the whole Terror shit. It wasn't worth explaining.

"Have you ever been in love, Kimora?" he asked me, and I swallowed hard.

"No, not all. Have you?"

"Nah."

"Who is the chick? I know you got somebody, Prince, you're too damn handsome not to."

He laughed.

"Man, look, I got somebody, but she ain't *it* for me. If she was *it*, I wouldn't be sitting here with you right now."

"Oh, well maybe I shouldn't be sitting here with you. You're probably lying. That's what men do." I rolled my eyes at him

"Man, hush that shit up. I told you if she was my woman, my girl, or anything close to being my wife, I wouldn't be sitting here with you. I don't lie. I don't like liars, so I definitely would tell you if I was a taken man."

"Don't tell me to shut up either." I rolled my eyes at him.

He chuckled as he grabbed my hand off the table. He held onto it and kissed the back of it.

"Have you ever truly been happy," he asked me, and I shook my head.

I have never known what it felt like to be genuinely happy. If it wasn't one thing, it was another.

"Me either. Maybe we can help each other find happy, ya know?"

"How can you make me happy?"

"Fuck with me and find out," he bragged.

I smirked. That sounded good, but with the shit I had planned, I didn't know how this was gonna work out. I liked Prince, and I never saw him in that light before, but now things are gonna be different between us. I could feel it.

Me and Prince finished our dinner, and afterward, he took me back home. I was all smiles as I floated to my bedroom. I never saw him in that light before, but after kissing him, and him asking me out on a date I knew for sure it could be something good between us.

MY CELL WAS RINGING, BREAKING ME OUT OF MY SLEEP. I grabbed it off the nightstand, and it read Prince. We'd been talking and texting, but I hadn't kicked it with him since he took me out to dinner. My mind was on other shit. I liked Prince, but I needed my head to stay in the game. And right now, my sights were on Terror.

I got out of bed and decided to take a shower. I needed to get my head together. He was dead ass wrong for leaving me that night at the restaurant, and I hadn't heard from him again. Since he wanted to act that way, I decided I was gonna take matters into my hands. I wasn't done with him yet.

After showering and dressing, I left the house and hopped in my ride. Jessica called my phone as I drove to my location.

"Hey, Jessie," I answered through the Bluetooth speaker.

"Hey, where did you run off to this morning?"

"I had to meet someone," I told her, and she exhaled deeply.

I rolled my eyes, but I didn't say anything in response.

"Kimora, what are you doing? Are you okay?"

"I'm fine. Why did you ask me that?"

"Because I'm …I'm just concerned about the way you've been moving lately. This is not like you at all."

"I'm good, Jessie, I need to holla at Knox. That's all," I told her

"Well, okay. Call me if you need me, I'm going to be home all day," she said.

After hanging up with Jessica, I pulled up to Terror's

mansion. I turned off my car as I saw the two soldiers he had standing guard in front of the house.

I walked up, and they tried to stop me before I could knock on his front door.

"Can you tell him Kimora is here to see him?" I said.

One of the dudes spoke into a walkie talkie to let him know what I said. He agreed to allow me to enter. When I went inside, I was led to his dining room where he was seated with a big ass pit bull on the side of him.

"Hello, beautiful." He smirked at me, and I smiled sheepishly.

"Hey."

"What can I do for you today?" he asked, and I chuckled. This nigga was truly a character.

"I came to see you. You haven't been answering any of my calls."

"Oh, I haven't?" he questioned with a laugh.

"No, you haven't."

"I don't talk to disrespectful women," he spat, and I just looked at him.

Terror was a fine older man, but I could see the evil behind his eyes.

"And how was I disrespectful to you? As I recall, you were the one who left me," I stated with a roll of the eyes.

"Talking to another man while in my presence was very disrespectful, sweetheart," he stated.

"Well, if you take that as disrespect, then I'm sorry. I didn't mean to disrespect you," I said, giving in to what he really wanted from me.

"A submissive woman. I like that." He grinned as he got out of his seat and came toward me

"Danger! Come 'here, boy," he barked at the dog, and the pit bull rushed to his side.

I was a little spooked because I didn't do dogs at all.

"Pat him," he demanded.

"I don't do dogs," I said.

"I said pat him, sweetheart." He smirked, and I did what he said as an eerie feeling crept up on me.

After patting the dog, Terror instructed the dog to run off. I stood there nervous as I didn't know what to do.

"Come on, let's go to the bedroom, sweetheart," he said.

I was starting to hate the word sweetheart. I followed him up the long spiral staircase to his bedroom. I was amazed at his big ass house. It was way bigger than Jessica's house.

When we got to his bedroom, he opened the door, and I went inside. I didn't wanna have sex with him because I was technically still a virgin.

"Sit down," he demanded, pointing at the bed, and I did as he said.

"So, tell me, Kimora. Why are you here? Are you here setting me up for my bitch ass brother?" he spewed with a frown.

"What? No... No, not at all," I said in a shaky tone.

"Then why the fuck were you with Prince?" he angrily questioned me.

"He's... he's my brother's best friend."

"Is that right?"

"Yes, that's right," I replied, and then he took his large hand and smacked the shit out of me.

Tears raced to my eyes, and in that moment, I knew I was in over my head. I bit off more than I could chew. Terror was certified crazy.

"Don't lie to me, bitch," he growled.

"I'm not lying!" I screeched, holding the side of my face.

"WHY THE FUCK ARE YOU HERE?" he shouted again.

"Because I want you... I wanna be here with you! I like you, Terror, and you're pushing me away," I explained.

I couldn't back out now. He wasn't having it. I was gonna either end up seriously hurt or dead.

"Then prove it," he spat, looking at me as if I was lying somehow.

"How?"

"Take off your pants and let me see your pussy," he exclaimed. I was shocked, but I knew it would come eventually. I swallowed hard and did as he said. I sat on his bed with my legs wide open, showing him my pussy.

"Now play with it," he demanded, still mean mugging me.

I did as he said. I played with myself, willing myself not to enjoy it like I had so many times before in the privacy of my own home.

Terror walked closer to me as he undid his pants. He pulled out his dick and slowly stroked it. Then he got up on me and placed the tip of his dick by my mouth. I've never sucked dick before, so I really didn't know what to do.

"Suck it, and if you bite me, I'm gonna slap you again,

sweetheart. Now, do it right so daddy can be satisfied," he stated.

Willing myself not to cry, I opened my mouth and slowly started sucking his dick. I tried my best not to bite him. I didn't want him to wild out and beat me because I wouldn't be able to handle it.

He started to moan, and I guess that was a good thing. I was doing something right.

"Don't move," he growled as I caught a rhythm.

I stayed still, and he started to pump in my mouth, going in and out feverishly.

"Ahhhh, fuck, you dirty bitch," he growled as he pumped himself in and out of my mouth.

Within seconds, I felt something thick, slimy, and salty shoot into my mouth. I was instantly grossed out. He pulled himself out of my mouth, and I was holding his semen. He looked at me and laughed.

"Swallow it," he demanded.

I closed my eyes and cringed as I swallowed his nut. I couldn't believe what I had gotten myself into.

"You say you want me. Now you got me. You belong to me, Kimora. Don't get it twisted anymore. Don't disrespect me again by talking to another man in my presence. I don't give a fuck who he is. Every time I see you, I want you to have on a dress that highlights your legs. And no panties on. You're my woman now, is that understood?"

I didn't say anything. I only nodded my head.

"I can't hear your voice. You said this is what you want, right?" He grinned.

"I understand, Jamie."

"It's not Jamie, it's daddy to you." He grinned and walked out of his bedroom.

Tears fell from my eyes as I thought about how he had degraded me as a woman. At that moment, I realized I might have just fucked up.

I'M ROCKING TILL THE WHEELS
FALL OFF

PRINCE

I couldn't stop thinking about Kimora as I sat in the studio listening to my homie, Benz. He was hot as shit on this rapping shit, and the money we were making out in the streets, we were trying to invest into a studio. I never knew how dope Kimora was until I got to be up under her. I tried my hardest to not let her get into my head, but I couldn't help it. I was digging her, and hard as fuck at that.

"Aye, bruh, you goin to Gangsta's coming home party tonight?" Benz asked, coming out of the booth and breaking my concentration.

I looked up at him and nodded.

"What's good, bro bro? You cool?" he asked.

"Yeah, my nigga, I'm good. Just got some shit on my mind," I told him.

"Who, Dana weird ass?" He chuckled, and I smirked.

Benz didn't like Dana for shit, and I didn't really know why.

"Nah, bruh. If I tell you some shit, you can't say shit to Knox."

"Nah, nigga, I ain't rocking like that. You know I ain't no fake ass nigga," he snarled.

"Man, it ain't shit like that. It's just that I ain't ready to tell the nigga yet."

"Man, what the fuck is it?"

"I been kicking it with Kimora."

"His sister, bruh?" he asked me.

"Yeah, man, you know who the fuck she is." I laughed at his dramatic ass.

"Yeah, I know… But damn, you know how that nigga feels about his damn sister. You want some problems, bruh." He shook his head, and I had to think about what he was saying. I knew that shit would cause problems, no doubt, but it is what it is.

"But here's the kicker, she's been kicking it with my brother, Terror," I told him, and his eyes widened.

"Get the fuck out of here, nigga. What kind of Steve Wilkos, Jerry Springer type of shit y'all got going on?"

"Man, fuck you. Shit is all complicated around here."

I shook my head because the shit did sound crazy, but I couldn't help how the fuck I felt at the moment.

"Hell, yeah that shit sounds complicated. Whatchu gonna do about Dana?"

"I'm still rocking with her too. Kimora ain't got her shit in order, and I'm just trying to see how this shit gonna rock. Ya feel me?"

"Nah, nigga, I don't, but all I'm gon' say is be careful fucking with that nigga Knox. I would hate to go to your funeral, bruh," he joked, but I wasn't worried about it. Knox wasn't the only nigga who could hold their own.

"Man, shut the fuck up. What time you sliding to the party tonight?" I asked him, switching the subject.

"Man, about eleven. You know that shit about to be lit. Everybody gonna be in that bitch." He grinned and laughed. This nigga was thirsty as fuck.

Me and Benz chopped it up in the studio until we parted ways. I went to Dana's crib, and I fucked her brains out to release some fucking stress. Afterward, I lay in the bed with my thoughts running a thousand miles per hour. I looked over at Dana, and she was snoring loudly. The dick always put her to sleep.

I grabbed my cell off the nightstand and dialed Kimora's number. I wasn't worried about Dana waking up because she was a heavy sleeper. The phone rang and rang in my ear. It was to the point that I got irritated just thinking about it. Instead of copiously trying to call, I got out of bed and went in the bathroom. I started the shower and hopped in it. Fuck it, I was gonna get dressed and head to the party. I needed something to take my mind off shawty's ass.

YFN Lucca's "Every Day We Lit" blasted through the club speakers as me and Benz made our way inside. I had hit up Knox, but the nigga didn't wanna roll out tonight. He was too busy trying to win Spirit back after that bitch,

Gianna, popped up at his crib. Whack shit. We headed toward the VIP section and sat down.

I ordered two bottles of Henny from the waitress, and my eyes scanned the crowd for the who's who. The whole hood was in attendance for this nigga, Gangsta. Gangsta was a nigga who I knew coming up on the low end. We were the same age, but the nigga acted as if he was about forty-five or some shit already. A cool ass nigga, but he was a killer. His name definitely represented him.

Him and his homies were known for robbing niggas, but they were feared in our hood because of how they came off. I respected the niggas, but like I said earlier, I wasn't worried.

"How you doing, baby? Do you need anything else?" the waitress asked as she set the bottles of Hennessey on the table in front of me.

"Nah, I'm good, baby, but if I need you, I'll make sure I find you." I winked at her and handed her the money for the liquor and a tip.

"Why the fuck you tip her all of that, bruh?" Benz asked once she was out of earshot.

"Nigga, how the fuck do you tip? Because that was definitely not a lot of bread. The fuck, nigga?" I laughed.

"Shit, that hoe would've got five dollars. Fuck that, man. A BJ too fucking much for these bucket head hoes."

"Nigga, you a fool." I laughed and poured myself a drink.

My eyes scanned the crowd again, something I did out of instinct, or better yet, something that I do when I don't trust my surroundings. I spotted an entourage of muthafuckas coming through the door. I frown my face when I spotted

Terror and Kimora. He was holding her hand, and she looked so out of place. This wasn't the type of shit for her. She didn't vibe with this club scene at all.

This nigga, I thought. I didn't wanna get in my feelings about her, but I definitely didn't like what I was seeing. I tossed my drink back and zoned out, trying to forget that Kimora and Terror were even in the building.

Terror's entourage was escorted to the largest seating area in the club because he had all these muthafuckas with him. I couldn't take my eyes off Kimora. Her hair was swept over her shoulder in a long braid, and her round face had a dark lipstick on it. She was dressed in a red dress that highlighted her firm, thick legs. I swear I wanted to kill Terror just because his arms were wrapped around her shoulders. I still couldn't figure out what she saw in the old ass nigga. Fuck that, it had to be something about his ass.

Terror's eyes connected with mine, and he grabbed Kimora's face and kissed her aggressively while still eyeing me. The scene made my stomach queasy. This was how much I despised my fucking brother.

I looked away and decided to sit back, relax, and enjoy the party. Fuck it, that's who she chose. I got drunk with Kimora on my mind the entered time. No matter what I said, I couldn't shake the thought of her.

I felt the urge to piss after a while, so I got up and headed for the bathroom. As I walked to the bathroom, I stopped in my tracks when I spotted Kimora coming my way. She hadn't noticed me yet.

I watched her walk into the women's bathroom, and I

followed her. I entered the women's bathroom, and Kimora looked back at me with wide eyes.

"What the hell?" she screeched. There weren't any more women around, and I liked that.

"Why you ain't been answering a nigga's calls?" I asked, walking up to her.

"I've been busy."

"You ain't been that fucking busy," I growled, pulling her close to me. She smelled so fucking good.

"Prince, whatchu doing? You know I'm here with Terror," she whispered, peeking over her shoulder.

She was nervous as hell as she thought about somebody coming into the bathroom. But that shit didn't matter to me. I pushed her against the wall and kissed her neck gently then kissed her lips. She stared me in the eyes and groaned.

"Pr...."

"Shh, I've been thinking about you. Stop ignoring my phone calls. When I call, you answer, aight?"

I eyed her, and she nodded.

"Alright, Prince, but let me go before he comes looking for me. I'll call you tonight when I make it home."

"You missed me, Mora?" I asked her in a husky tone, and she rolled her eyes.

"I don't, but I do." She giggled.

I leaned in and kissed her on her lips one time and walked out, grinning the entire time as I headed back to the section I was in with Benz.

WHEN LOVE CALLS YOUR NAME

KIMORA

"Mora! Mora!" Jessica screamed my name.

I came out of my bedroom and met her at the top of the stairs.

"Yes?" I screamed.

"You have a visitor," she spewed, frowning at me.

I didn't mean to take my anger out on her, but I was worn out. I swallowed hard, and nervousness overtook my body as I thought about it being Terror waiting for me at the door.

When I got downstairs, it was Prince sitting in the living room. I was nervous to look at him. He was so damn fine, it was sickening. Me and Prince still had been texting, but I wasn't trying to go anywhere near serious with him.

I had been with Terror for the last two weeks, and this

was the first time I was able to go home since he was out of town for a business meeting.

"What's up, baby?" He smiled as he hugged me.

"Hey, Prince." I smiled.

"What's up with you? Why you ain't been trying to get with a nigga?" he asked me.

"Prince, I told you I was chilling with Terror," I told him, and he laughed.

"You can't be serious, man. Terror's old ass got a hold on you for real, huh?"

I couldn't tell him what I was really feeling. How this was all a part of my plan.

"Yeah, he does."

"Wait... What the fuck..." He frowned then grabbed my face and turned it side to side.

"This bitch ass nigga hitting you now, Kimora?" he asked.

I shook my head. It was true, Terror was putting his hands on me every chance he got. He was crazy and sadistic. Terror slapped me if I didn't answer him right away, he slapped me if I didn't suck his dick right. He didn't even want pussy, he only liked his dick sucked, and he wanted to watch me play with my pussy. He never wanted to actually fuck me. He said my mouth couldn't get pregnant. He claimed he fucked up one time when he was younger and got some chick pregnant, and he refused to do it again. He claimed kids were nothing but brats and headaches.

Being with him for these last two weeks had really shown me how crazy he really is. He really didn't have all his marbles there, but I refused to let him win. I wanted Terror to suffer for everything he had done to my family.

I wanted to take his ass out from the inside. I don't know why I had this evilness in me, but that was just how I felt. Everyone who tried to destroy me or tried to manipulate me in any way needed to pay for my pain. I was hell bent on revenge, and not even God himself could stop me.

Looking at Prince, I felt a sort of calm around him. He was different, and I liked that. The good morning texts and good night phone calls were everything to me, but I knew I couldn't move forward with dating him while I was doing this shit.

Y'all might think I'm crazy for this, but I went crazy a long time ago. I made a vow that I was gonna do what I had to do if I got the chance.

"It's nothing, Prince. I swear, it's nothing," I told him, and he shook his head.

"I bet Knox don't know this shit either, huh?" he barked.

"Once again, I'm grown. Please don't get my brother in my business with Terror. Knox can't afford to go back to jail. I will handle things my own way, and in my own time."

"Kimora, whatchu doing, man? This isn't making any sense to me," he said.

"I'm doing what I have to do, Prince."

"What the fuck does that shit mean?"

"Nothing... Look, I'm tired, and I don't feel like talking right now. So, just go."

"I ain't going no fucking where. I ain't liking how you moving. You don't want me to tell Knox, but you flirting with danger. I'm feeling you, Kimora, and you tryna run away from a nigga. I don't fold easily. So, like I said, I ain't going nowhere," he spat and headed for the stairs.

I looked at him like he was crazy, but I followed him. Once he was up the stairs, he went to my bedroom like he knew exactly which one it was, kicked off his sneakers, and climbed in the bed.

"Prince, really?" I eyed him, and he didn't respond as he grabbed the remote control to my television and turned on the TV.

I let out a deep sigh and closed my bedroom door. I sat on the edge of the bed and stared at him.

"You're crazy," I whispered, and he laughed.

"I know," he replied, pulling me to him and kissing the top of my forehead.

He tried to kiss my lips, but I turned my head. I couldn't dare kiss him on the lips after what I'd been doing with Terror. He didn't get offended. Instead, he kissed me on my neck and wrapped his arms around my waist as we spooned and watched TV. I felt at peace in his arms, and I didn't know why. This shit with Prince was coming on too strong for me, and I didn't think I was ready for the word *love*.

The next day, Prince wouldn't leave easily, so I was sitting at the lake with him while he did his fishing. I actually enjoyed the time I was spending with him. We were getting closer, and that scared me.

"I didn't think black men went fishing," I told Prince as we sat in front of the pond and he held his fishing rod in his hand.

He looked back at me and smirked.

"Nah, who told you some dumb shit like that?" he asked, and I cracked up laughing.

"No one. It just doesn't seem like a black man's sport. Maybe basketball, but not fishing."

"It's not a sport, sweetheart. It's a hobby, and it brings me peace."

I hated the way the word sweetheart rolled off his tongue. The minute he said it, I thought about Terror's sadistic ass.

"Oh, okay." I didn't say anything else after that.

"What brings you peace, Mora?"

"Huh?"

"You heard me, what brings you peace?" he asked again. I couldn't answer that because honestly, I didn't have anything that brought me peace of mind.

"Nothing," I responded just above a whisper.

Prince dropped his fishing rod and came over to the picnic table that I was sitting on. He stood between my legs and looked me in my eyes. The way he stared at me was so damn intense. I looked away, but he turned my face back to his.

"You gotta stop letting life beat you up, ma. You know that, right?"

My eyes watered, and I willed myself not to cry, but I couldn't help it because he was right,

"I know."

"Do you, baby? I mean, I know shit has been rough for you, but you don't break down and crumble, Ma. You better start living yo best life. We ain't guaranteed to be here forever, and making yaself miserable on a daily because things didn't pan out how you wanted them to ain't cool."

"I hear you, Prince."

"Do you hear me? Or you just saying that? You too fucking beautiful to be going through the shit you going through. I don't even wanna bring up my brother's name, but man, I hope you stopped fucking with him because he ain't right, bruh."

"I did," I lied to him.

It wasn't his business what I was doing when it came to Terror. I wanted that nigga wrapped around my finger, I wanted him to beg me for his life when I snatched it from him.

"Don't lie to me, Kimora," he snapped. He knew I was lying.

"I'm not, Prince."

He gave me a look like I better not be.

"I'm digging you, shawty, and I want you to know that shit. I don't know how Knox will feel about us, but I'm willing to bet he won't have a problem with it."

"Ain't no us until you get rid of whatever her name is," I told him, and he laughed.

"I'm gonna take care of that real soon, believe me."

"Okay, Prince." I eyed him.

He leaned in and kissed my lips. I wrapped my arms around his neck, pulling him closer to me. We fell backward on the picnic table while engaged in a lip lock. He slid his tongue in my mouth, and I started to get wet. I was never turned on sexually, so this was definitely feeling good.

His slid his hands in my leggings, and I tensed up. I

didn't want him to touch me. Terror didn't touch me; he only required that I touch myself. Prince broke our kiss and stared into my eyes.

"Let go, baby," he whispered, and I only stared back.

My breathing was heavy, and my eyes were low. We were in broad daylight in the middle of the lake, surrounded by nothing but trees, grass, and fucking bugs, and still, I was nervous.

"I'm not gonna hurt you, Mora," he whispered, and I slowly let go.

I dropped my legs, and he slid off my yoga pants. I was wearing a light pink thong panty, and he bit his bottom lip as he stared at me. I couldn't believe I was about to fuck him in this park. He stared down at me, and I shivered from the breeze since I was bare at the bottom.

He grabbed the bag we had with food in it and took the strawberries out. He stuck the cool strawberries by my opening, and I jumped from the coolness, causing him to chuckle.

"Let me taste that pussy, baby," he whispered in a husky tone.

"No, no, it's fine. You don't have to do that," I chimed, sitting up, but Prince took his hand and pushed me back on the picnic table.

Nervousness ran through my body because I never had oral sex before or sex at all, and this was gonna be a different feeling for me.

He slid my panties off and spread my legs on the picnic table. I was so nervous thinking somebody was gonna walk up and catch us, but the nervousness faded away the moment I felt his tongue connect with my pussy.

"Ahhhhhh." I moaned as he licked slowly around my pussy, kissed the inside of my thighs, and then connected with my clit.

"Ohhhhhhh baby… ahhhh," I cried as he twirled his tongue around my clit, sucking it gently.

The shit felt so fucking good. It was a feeling I never had before.

"Ohhhhhhh, Prince… Ooohhhh baby," I cried.

Prince sucked and slurped on my pussy until my legs were shaking uncontrollably. Another thing I have never felt before. Even when I masturbated, the feeling was never like this. Once he was done, he came up for air, and my juices were glistening around his mouth. He had a smirk etched on his face, and I was so embarrassed that I couldn't look at him.

"Whatchu looking crazy for? You didn't think I could make that pussy scream? You liked that shit, didn't you?" he whispered, wiping his mouth with his t shirt that he had taken off.

"I did," I replied with a smirk on my face.

I was still sitting there with a bare ass because I honestly couldn't move. My legs had shaken so damn badly, it was miracle that they weren't broke.

"I know you did. I liked tasting that pussy," he whispered and kissed my lips.

Damn this man was sexy as fuck to me.

"I'm gonna make sure you feel good every chance I get. I wanna get you right, ma, so we can be together. You know, I wanna show how you are supposed to be treated. I just wanna be that nigga, yo nigga."

"You can be, Prince, it just takes time."

"But you gotta stop fucking with this nigga Terror. You lied to me, and I know you did, but that doesn't stop how I'm feeling you. Just don't lie to me anymore, Kimora. And break the shit off with him ASAP," he snapped, and I nodded.

"Now, come here and let me show you how to fish," he chimed.

His bare chest was cut up, and he had so many damn tattoos. I loved his walk, his talk, his curly fro that was faded on the sides, his juicy lips. Everything about Prince was sexy to me.

I got off the picnic table and slid back on my yoga pants. He grabbed my thong panties and placed them in his back pocket.

"What are you doing?"

"I'm taking these with me." He grinned, and I shook my head.

Prince and I chilled by the lake fishing, talking, and kissing for the rest for the day. When I made it home, I was floating on cloud nine. I hadn't felt this good in a while. For the first time in a long time, I hadn't thought about Terror's ass.

I STAYED WITH PRINCE FOR THREE DAYS, AND WHEN I FINALLY was able to break away, I slept like there was no tomorrow.

When I woke up this morning, I had a thousand missed calls from Terror. When Terror called my phone last night after me and Prince came from the lake after fishing, I wanted to answer, but Prince snatched my phone out of my hands and turned it off. And I left it that way. I mean, I was having such a proper time with him, and I didn't need any interruptions.

I went downstairs, and Jessica was in the kitchen making breakfast. She looked up at me and then back down at her skillet. This was the first time I'd seen her pissed at me.

"What did I do?" I asked.

"I don't like how you're moving, Kimora," she snapped.

"How I'm moving? What do you mean?"

"I mean all the secrets, all the running around. I don't know what's on your agenda, but you need to be careful. Something is telling me that something is gonna go terribly wrong. I'm not your mother, and I'm not trying to preach to you like I am. But please... please... be careful."

"I told you I am. I'm fine, Jessica. I swear I am."

"Then why is your skin bruised? Why are you dealing with a man who hits you?" she asked me.

I swallowed hard. I didn't think she saw it.

"You didn't think I would notice, huh?" She smirked.

"No," I replied honestly.

"Well, I did, and I don't like it. I have friends in high places, Kimora, and all you gotta do is say the word, and that bastard will be under the jail."

I had to laugh seeing Jessica getting gangsta.

"I got it. I'm good, I promise, Jessie," I assured her and kissed her on the cheek.

I finished eating my breakfast then showered and got dressed for the day. Jessica was gone to work by the time I finished dressing. I grabbed my car keys because Knox texted me and told me he wanted to do lunch with me. As I came down the stairs, I stopped in my tracks when I saw the two big, burly ass bodyguards waiting by my front door.

"What the hell?" I shouted and dropped my keys to the marble floor.

"Sweetheart, come inside," Terror's deep voice boomed out.

I rounded the corner to the living room, and he was sitting on my living room couch. Jessica was sitting on the couch next to him with a security guard aiming a gun at her head. I thought she had left when I heard the alarm chirp on the house. Tears welled up in my eyes at the sight before me, and I knew then I had messed up by letting Prince turn my phone off last night.

"Sweetheart, didn't I say you were mine? Didn't I say never to ignore me?" he growled, giving me a menacing look.

I didn't respond as I stared at him. He must be out of his mind.

"You wouldn't want me to harm the pretty lady now, would you?" he asked as he rubbed the side of Jessica's face, and she trembled with fear.

"No... No, Terror, please don't hurt her," I begged.

"What did you just call me?"

"I'm sorry... I... I mean Daddy... Daddy, please don't hurt her," I cried.

"Ahhhh, that's more like it." He grinned and then he motioned for the guard to remove his gun from Jessica's head.

"Now gather your things and let's go," he demanded, and I swallowed hard.

Terror got off the couch and walked up on me. He looked me in my eyes while a sinister grin was etched on his face, and then he did what he did best. He slapped the hell out of me, causing me to fall to the floor.

"Get up, and let's go! You disobedient bitch!" he snapped, grabbing me by my hair off the floor and leading me out the front door.

I cried as he dragged me to his black Escalade. Trey's bitch ass was standing guard at the back door, and he opened the door with a big ass grin on his face. He liked watching me in pain.

Terror threw me in the back seat of the truck, and he got in next to me. The guard started up the ignition and peeled off. I looked out the window and cried the entire time. Jessica was standing in the doorway crying buckets, and I knew at that moment I should've taken her advice.

MESSY BITCHES

KNOX

As I drove around the city with my Glock .40 on my lap, my nostrils flared in irritation. I had just gotten off the phone with Jessica, the chick Kimora was staying with, and she had told me what happened between Kimora and Terror. First off, I didn't even know my sister was talking to some fucking dude. On top of that, it was Prince's older brother, who was old enough to be our fucking daddy. And thirdly, this nigga was putting his fucking hands on my sister. I was fucking heated.

This nigga didn't have a clue who he was fucking with. I would die for mine. I didn't give a fuck how many niggas he had on his squad. Little did these niggas know, being in the joint, I've gotten to know niggas too, and I was a thoroughbred ass nigga. Muthafuckas were gonna ride for me just because I was that nigga.

My cell vibrated on my lap, and when I picked it up, it was Prince. I'd been calling the nigga since I got off the phone with Jessica. I wanted his brother and ASAP.

"Yo?" I answered.

"What's good, my nigga?"

"Man, what the fuck is your brother's address?" I barked into the phone.

"Why? What's up, nigga? You good?" he questioned.

"Nah, I ain't good. That nigga done snatched up Twin, putting his hands and shit on her. Man, where the fuck is this nigga," I growled.

"Nigga, where you at? I'm about to ride with you."

"Nah, my nigga, I don't trust you like that. That's yo blood, and you might be riding with that nigga. Fuck that," I told him honestly.

"Nigga you coming at me like that? You know I don't fuck with that nigga! You know that shit, Knox! I only got two brothers, you and Benz! Nothing more and nothing less. I don't fuck with that bitch ass lunatic," he shouted, and I exhaled.

"Nigga, I'm riding down 43rd street. Where you at?" I asked, giving in.

"I'm at Mom's crib, come and scoop me."

"Aight, I'm on my way right now," I told him and hung up the phone.

I wouldn't hesitate to lay Prince bitch ass down if he tried to be on some fluky shit. That old ass nigga, Terror, was about to catch this hot shit, and that's on my momma.

When I pulled up to Prince's mom's spot, Prince hopped in the ride. We dapped each other up, and he told me the address to his brother's crib. I put the pedal to the metal to get to Twin as fast as I could. I had so many thoughts running through my mind about why she wouldn't tell me she was fucking with this dude. Nothing about her situation made any sense to me.

When we pulled up to his house, it was empty. There were no cars out front, no guards, no nothing. I looked at Prince like he was on some bullshit.

"You sure this is the muthafucking house?" I snarled.

"Man, I know where the fucking nigga lives," he snapped back.

"Well, it looks like he doesn't fucking live here anymore," I growled.

"Man, shut the fuck up, and let's wait it out," he suggested, and that's what we did.

It was pointless. By midnight, the nigga, Terror, still hadn't come home. I was so frustrated that I peeled away from his crib and dropped Prince off without saying a word to him.

I drove off like a bat out of hell, and I was frustrated as fuck to say the least. I wanted my fucking sister, and I wanted her ASAP. This nigga was not allowing her to answer her phone, and that pissed me off even fucking more.

I decided to call her again this time, even though I knew she probably wouldn't answer. I was confused, and for some reason, I felt like I was alone. The phone rang in my ear three times, and just when I was about to hang up, Kimora's sultry voice came through.

"Hey, Bruh Bruh." She sounded dry like she was asleep.

"What the fuck is good? Where you at, man?" I barked into the phone.

"I'm at a friend's house," she responded, and I was instantly pissed that she lied to me.

"Who the fuck is yo friend? Huh? You ain't got no muthafucking friends, Kimora! You with that old ass nigga Terror, ain't you?" I barked.

"Yes, but I'm good, Bruh Bruh. Why you hollering?"

"Because you weren't answering yo fucking phone! The fuck you think!" I shouted at her while she wanted to play shit off like everything was kosher.

"I wasn't answering because I was busy. That's all, Bruh Bruh. I'm sorry for not answering, but I'm good. I swear I am."

'That's not what the fuck Jessica told me. She said niggas ran up in her shit with guns and shit, and that bitch ass nigga hit you. So, she's lying on you, Kimora?"

"No... No, Knox! Look, I'm good. I'll call you when I leave here," hhe hurriedly said and hung up the phone in my face.

"Fuck! Fuck!" I shouted as I hit my steering wheel over and over again.

I was fucking pissed.

THE NEXT DAY, I COULDN'T GET KIMORA OFF MY MIND. I needed to see and hear from my fucking sister. I knew I wouldn't be able to rest until I got in touch with her. I called and called her phone, but I never got an answer.

I was sitting outside of Spirit's crib. Besides Kimora, she was the next person I couldn't stop thinking about. I felt fucked up that Gianna pulled that goofy ass shit popping up at my crib like shit was sweet when it wasn't.

I watched her house, and I hesitated before I got out of my car and headed for the door. I just wanted to talk to her and explain to her how sorry I was for that bullshit.

After debating with myself, I finally got out the car and headed for her door. I knocked heavily on her front door, and she came to open it. She had on one of those bonnet things chicks like to wear, some joggers, and a thin ass tank top that showcased her big, round nipples. I had to catch myself from licking my lips as I eyed her body up and down.

"What do you want, Knox?" she asked, rolling her eyes at me.

"You."

"*Tuh!* I can't tell." She scoffed.

"I don't know how you can't tell, as much as I've been calling you, popping up at the club, and sweating you. You got me out here like a fucking stalker, man."

"Shit, you should know all about stalkers, like that bitch who popped up at your house. Knox, that wasn't cool at all," she stated.

She was right, but for some reason, Gianna felt like she was entitled to me.

"I'm sorry about that, ma, and that shit won't ever happen again."

"How do I know that? I've dealt with that already, and I don't wanna go back to it. I'm sick and tired of that type of shit."

"Stop comparing me to all these other clowns you fucked with. I'm one of a kind, baby, and you know it, so be cool with that shit. I'm apologizing, Spirit. Damn, what I gotta do to make you understand that this was all a misunderstanding."

"Who is she, Knox?"

"She's somebody I fucked with while I was in the joint. She wrote me letters, sent me nudes, put money on my books, came to visit me, when I had nobody. So yeah, I was fucking with her, but we also made it clear that I was a single man."

"Well, it looks as if she got that shit twisted."

"Yeah, she did, but at the same time, I made it very clear the night you left. I'm out here begging, and you interrogating my ass like I'm on *The First 48*. What's up with that shit, Spirit?" I eyed her, but she wasn't budging.

She was staring at me with the screw face, and her arms were folded across her chest.

"Whatever, Knox. Fuck you. You're probably lying," she spat and tried to close the door in my face, but I stuck my foot in the door to stop her.

She looked at me like I was crazy or some shit. I wasn't, but she wasn't about to disrespect me like that. Nah, fuck that. I didn't know who Spirit thought she was fucking with when it came to this shit. I pushed the door open with all my might and pushed her against the wall. She looked at me with bucked eyes.

"Don't ever try to close a fucking door in my face," I spat, looking down at her.

"You think that tough guy shit works on me? I'm not scared of you," she argued, and I smirked at her pretty ass.

"And I don't want you to be, baby. I'm not trying to hurt you," I whispered and kissed her lips.

She tried to turn her head away from me, but I grabbed it roughly and held it in place. I kissed her lips again, this time more aggressively.

"Let me go, Knox. You can't force nobody to be with you," she screamed, turning her head away from mine.

I slid my tongue in her mouth and my hands between her legs. Finding her honey pot, I flicked my finger back and forth against her clit. She moaned in pleasure as I began to kiss her neck.

I stripped Spirit out of her clothing right there at the doorway and fucked her against the wall. She clawed my back so fucking good my shit was burning. I needed a way to release my frustrations, and what better way than to punish the fucking pussy. Shit was A-1, and I was falling more in love with her than she knew.

Afterward, we lay spent in her bed spent, both of us staring at the ceiling. I was smoking a blunt and we both were quiet.

"I'm still not fucking with you," she said, and I chuckled.

"Man, you wish. You got me forever, ma. Stop fighting it. That's my pussy, that's my body, and as of today, you're done working at that fucking club. No more. I can provide you with anything you need. Finish school, man, and do yo damn thing. That strip club shit ain't you. Never was," I told her as I inhaled the blunt one more time.

"Knox, why do you want me? Why you checking for me this hard? You don't even understand my life and the mistakes I have made. If you knew all about me, then you wouldn't want me. I promise you wouldn't," she said, and that made me look at her ass funny.

"Man, kill that noise. I'm grown. I know what the fuck I want, baggage and all. Now shut the fuck up and hit the blunt. My dick getting hard again, and I want you to ride this muthafucka," I told her, which I meant.

"Knox, stop telling me to shut the fuck up. I hate the way you talk sometimes. It's so damn rude."

"Aight, aight, my bad. Can you be quiet, Spirit, because you blowing my high, and I wanna still make love. Because that's what we're doing, making love, so we can make some babies. I want some babies, and I want them by you," I told her.

She looked at me and burst into laughter.

"I swear, you are certifiable crazy, my nigga." She giggled as I passed her the blunt

"Yeah, yeah, that's what they all say," I replied as we got high and talked about everything under the sun.

We didn't even have sex again, only slept in each other's arms. She felt so right lying against my chest, and I knew without a doubt that she was the one for me. I didn't give a fuck about her flaws because everybody had them.

"Awwww, hell nawl!!!"

I heard a voice in my sleep, but I didn't open my eyes because I felt like I needed to lie there for a few more seconds.

"Hell No! Knox, wake the fuck up! Wake up, nigga!" Spirit's voice boomed out.

I slowly opened my eyes, and the sun peeking through her bedroom window caused me to squint.

"What's wrong, man?" I was confused and still tired as fuck.

"That crazy bitch just busted my living room window out, Knox! No, fuck that! Get yo ass up and get that bitch, Knox!" she screamed.

I hopped up, hoping Gianna's stupid ass didn't do no shit like that. And how in the fuck did she know where the fuck Spirit lived in the first fucking place?

"Bitch, you tried it, hoe!" Spirit yelled as she placed sneakers on her feet. Her bonnet was still on, and she only had on my big t-shirt.

"Yo, YO, YO. What the fuck is going on, baby?" I put on my jeans and grabbed my gun.

When I walked to the living room, glass was every fucking where. Her largest window in the living room of the house was busted out. This bitch Gianna done went crazy.

While I was looking out the window to see if Gianna was still outside, I noticed that my car was leaning. I went outside to examine my fucking ride, and lo and behold, this bitch had put my fucking tires on a flat, and she did the same to Spirit's car.

"Spirit, get inside!" I called out to her as she tried to chase Gianna's car down the street looking crazy as hell. I understood, though.

"Knox, I'm done!! Until that bitch gets some control over

herself, leave me the fuck alone!" she screamed at me as she burst into tears.

"I don't have money to fix this shit! I just don't!" she sobbed, but she didn't have to worry about a thing because I didn't have paper in my pocket for nothing. I had her, she was definitely gonna be good.

"I gotchu. Don't worry about shit, bae. I promise I gotchu, and I'm so fucking sorry," I apologized to Spirit as I thought about ways to get Gianna's goofy ass back for this shit.

I WAS IRRITATED AS I WALKED INTO GIANNA'S APARTMENT. THAT goofy ass shit she pulled with Spirit was driving me crazy. Now, Spirit wasn't answering her phone for me or nothing like that since I've left her crib.

"Hey, bae." Gianna smiled.

As sexy and fine as her ass is, she was crazy as fuck, and I definitely didn't see the signs if that shit.

"Ain't no fucking, bae. How the fuck you know where my girl lives?" I growled, staring down at her.

"Your girl? When did she become your girl, Knox?" she asked with desperation laced in her voice.

"She's been my girl."

"You told me you didn't want anything exclusive."

"I didn't want anything with you exclusive!" I barked.

"Nigga, fuck you!" she spat and swung on me.

She slapped the shit out of me and tried to do it again, but I grabbed her arms and pinned her against the wall.

"Don't put ya fucking hands on me no more, or Imma break yo fucking wrist," I growled, and she gave me the puppy dog eyes.

"You chose her, but I was the bitch holding you down, putting money on your books, writing and sending you letters. It was me, not that hoe. And you gon' play me like this, Knox?"

"Gianna, you tripping, bruh... I let you know what it was the moment you asked me, and you said you understood that shit. You said you were down for a nigga either way."

"You ain't shit, nigga! Ain't shit, I swear! Let me the fuck go, Knox!" she screamed at me.

I laughed seeing her get so hyped up about nothing. I let her wrist go and stared at her. For her to be so damn sexy, she was a nut case.

"Look, man, let me go. I got a shawty now, and I can't fuck with you like that, Gianna. You were good to me, and that's why if you ever need me, I'll be there for you, but I ain't fucking with you on no other type of level."

"Fuck you, Knox! Get the fuck out of my apartment! And fuck that raggedy bitch too! She can't win! She ain't supposed to win! She's a stripper, Knox!" she squealed, and I had to do a double take.

She knew a lot about Spirit, and it was mind boggling.

"Shut the fuck up, Gianna. Worry about ya self. Out here thottin' it with old ass truck drivers. You thought I was gonna wife yo ass up after a nigga came in yo shit? Man, fuck out of here," I spat.

"And that stripper bitch gonna give yo ass AIDS, clown.

Who falls for a stripper?" she screamed, and I shook my head.

"Me! I'm in love with a stripper," I sang in my T-Pain voice and walked out of her apartment.

She slammed her door hard as fuck, and I laughed all the way to the elevator. Now, all I had to do was go get my woman back.

SHE GOT ME IN MY FEELINGS

PRINCE

Kimora wasn't answering her fucking phone, and it was pissing me off to no end. I hated when she did shit like this. After me and Knox did the stakeout that night in front of Terror's crib, I went back and sat in front of that muthafucka, and they still never came to his crib. That shit had my mind puzzled.

I knew she wasn't hurt or anything of that nature, but I wanted to see her, hear from her. I missed her ass like crazy.

Dana was sitting on the edge of the bed smoking her a blunt, and it was like every little thing that she said to me irritated me to no end. I didn't wanna be with her, but I had no choice since Kimora wasn't giving me the time of day.

I could still smell her pussy on my lips, and damn, she smelled so sweet. I didn't know what kind of bullshit she was on, fucking with this nigga, Terror, but I wished she would just let the shit go. Whatever it was wasn't worth it.

"What's up, boo? You okay?" Dana looked back at me.

"Yeah, I'm good, just thinkin'," I replied.

"Oh, you want me to make you feel better?"

She smirked and put the blunt out in the ashtray then climbed on the bed with me and got between my legs.

"Nah, I'm good, ma," I responded and moved her out the way.

I wasn't in the mood to be fucking with her right now. Sex wasn't everything to a nigga. I couldn't get off my mind how well me and Kimora vibed. She was like the ying to my yang.

"Damn, when you start not wanting to fuck?" She smacked her lips and glared at me.

"Didn't I tell you I had some shit on my mind? Damn, man, why the fuck you gotta be so damn difficult when it comes to shit?" I snapped.

Getting out of the bed and grabbing my cell, walked out the bedroom and went in the bathroom then plopped down on the toilet.

I scrolled through my contacts and came upon Kimora's name. I still hadn't received a text message back from her from when I texted her yesterday. Instead of texting again, I called her. The phone rang in my ear three times, and then she finally picked up.

"Hello?" She sounded groggy on the phone like she was sleep or something.

"What's up, man? Where you at?" I immediately asked, and she chuckled.

"In bed sleeping, Prince. How are you doing?"

"Not good, I've been hitting you up, and ya ass ain't responded to a nigga. Fuck is that about?" I asked her.

"I'm sorry. I've been busy."

"Busy doing what? You too busy you can't answer ya phone for a nigga?"

"Damn, I didn't think you were my man. I said I'm sorry. Shouldn't that be good enough?"

"It's not good enough. I wanna see you, and right now," I demanded, and she exhaled.

"Okay, let me get showered and dressed, and I'll meet you somewhere."

"Aight, man," I replied and hung up the phone.

A smirk came upon my face. I was happy as fuck that I was about to get a chance to see her. I missed her lil thick ass already.

I got off the toilet and went back in the bedroom. Dana was fully dressed. She was glaring at me with her arms folded across her chest.

"Why the fuck you looking like that?" I frowned.

"Get 'cho shit, and get the fuck out of my crib, Prince. You can go back to your momma's house for all I care. You too damn disrespectful!" she shouted, and I only stared at her.

"Dana, chill out with all that shit, man!" I snapped at her as I went and grabbed my clothes.

"Really, Prince! How the fuck you gonna be talking to some bitch while you laid up in my house. You too damn disrespectful. Fuck you! I want you gone!" she screamed, and I nodded.

I didn't argue with her. I simply got dressed and left her crib. I had enough bread to get my own spot anyway. I didn't wanna deal with moms, and Dana was good enough to get my dick wet, but I got tired of her ass at times.

I hopped in my ride and headed for Portillo's. I texted Kimora and told her where I was headed so she could meet me.

When I pulled up to Portillo's and hopped out my ride. Before I went inside, I spotted a jewelry shop. I went inside, and the sales lady asked me did I need any help. I spotted the his and hers watch collection that they had and asked could I see them.

Once they pulled the different ones out of the case, it was only one set that really caught my eye. The set was 20 G's which wasn't shit, but I was digging it. I wasn't ready to give Kimora a ring or no shit like that, but the watch was dope, and it was something that connected us to each other.

"I want those," I told the sales lady, and she grinned as she rang up the watches.

I looked at my phone, and Kimora had texted me and told me she was in Portillo's parking lot.

After the lady bagged up the watches, I headed outside and walked to her car. When I walked up to her window, her head was down, and she was looking in her phone.

"That's how niggas get robbed," I told her.

She looked up at me and smiled

"Whatever, Prince." She chuckled.

"You hungry?" I asked.

"Nah, not really. I ate what Jessica had fixed for breakfast."

"Oh, aight. I'm about to grab an Italian beef, and then we can bounce," I told her, and she eyed me.

"Bounce? Where we going?"

"We going wherever I say we going," I spat over my shoulder as I walked off.

I went in the restaurant and ordered my food. After retrieving my food, I got in my ride, and she followed me. I went to the Marriott hotel and checked into a room.

Me and Kimora sat on the bed while I ate my food. She was silent, and it was low key bothering me that she wasn't saying shit.

"What's up? You good?"

"Yeah, I'm fine… I just don't understand all of this ya know."

"What's there to understand? You here with me, and I'm here with you."

"You know what I mean, Prince. Me dealing with your brother and then you trying to deal with me. It's all too crazy, and I can't let myself get caught up in this type of shit."

"Man, you ain't gonna get caught up in nothing. I told you to stop fucking with the nigga. I don't see what's so hard about that. You let him come into Jessica's crib and shit. They roughed her up, and that shit wasn't right at all."

"I got this shit."

"You have what? Because, from the looks of things, it seems as if you don't have shit under control."

"I have an agenda, Prince. It's just something… I have to do."

"Man, yo ass sound crazy. Do you hear yourself

Kimora?"

"I do."

What else do you want from me? Because I can't give you all of me, no matter how hard I try. I just can't," she said in a low tone as tears clouded her eyes.

"I want you to give me a chance, ma, let me show you who the fuck I am."

"It's not you I'm worried about, though, Prince. It's me. I'm too damaged."

"Too damaged?"

"Yes! I need revenge. It's the only way I can see to make me feel better! I've tried and tried to let shit go, but I can't! I fucking can't!"

"Kimora! That shit doesn't make any sense to me."

"It's not for you to understand."

"How you tryna stop a nigga from loving you?"

"I've been so fucking broken that it doesn't make any sense. Pain broke me down, but revenge gave me life! Muthafuckas are gonna pay for my pain! And all you're doing is standing in my way. I don't need you! I didn't need a man to build me up! I built myself up! I didn't tell you to fall for me, you wanna know why? It's because I'm… I'm damaged, Prince. I know I won't be able to fully give you my heart. I can't do it because I don't know how. She snapped, and tears rolled down her face. If she thought that lil ass speech was gonna move me, she had another thing coming.

"Man, fuck all that you talking about! You gonna give me that shit 'cause I ain't taking no for an answer. I didn't need to ask you can I fall for you, and you ain't gotta need me, shorty, 'cause all that matters is that I need you. I ain't letting yo ass walk away from me. Shid, you don't want them problems, Mora. Man, look, I was stuck on you from the moment I met you, whether you wanna believe it or not. You ain't got no choice but to love a nigga 'cause I'm gonna love you until I'm in the dirt, ma, and that's real," I told her, and she shook her head.

"What are you doing to me, Prince?" she whispered.

"I'm trying to love you."

"You don't love me."

"Yeah, I do, and I know you love me. Now come here."

I nodded, and she stood up and came between my legs. I lifted her chin up so she could look me in my eyes.

"Kimora, stop tryna fight what we have for each other. Some shit is just meant to be, no matter how you try to slice it."

"Whatchu tryna ben my Prince charming or something?" she asked, and I chuckled.

"Shit, have you ever been kissed by a hood prince?" I asked her.

She laughed while shaking her head.

"Well, let me show you." I leaned in and gently kissed her lips.

Me and Kimora chilled in the hotel for two days straight, not once having sex, but I did taste that pussy a few times while we were there. I knew she was still fragile from when that nigga Trey tried to take advantage of her. She's never talked about that shit with me, but I knew what happened because of Knox. The entire time we chilled, Terror called her phone.

It looked like I was about to war with my brother over his girl and this money in these streets, but I didn't give a fuck. Whatever happens, happens. I wanted Kimora to myself.

"WHAT'S WRONG WITH YOU?" DANA ASKED AS WE DROVE TO my mother's house for a barbeque.

I looked at her and shook my head. I had started back fucking with Dana because Kimora kept playing mind games with a nigga. She had muthafuckas doing stake outs and shit, and she still didn't leave the nigga alone. I was tired of pouring out my feelings for her to still be up under this bitch ass nigga. I hadn't heard from her since we were at the hotel for those two days. She was like Houdini. One day she was there, and the next day she was gone, and I wasn't feeling the back and forth shit. She kept talking this revenge shit, but I didn't see it getting her nowhere fucking with a nigga like Terror.

"Nothing, I'm aight," I replied.

"You're being standoffish, Prince. You sure about that?" she questioned again.

"I'm positive, baby, just got some shit on my mind," I lied.

I couldn't stop thinking about Kimora's ass. I was hopeful that Terror would show up at mom's today with Kimora in tow because I knew that's who she was with. He never missed my mom's birthday. For some reason, that was the only thing he ever acknowledged about my mother.

I didn't know what the fuck was going on, but I needed to hear her voice like yesterday. This shit was on my mind too much. I hoped Terror ain't fucking hurt her because that shit will kill me. Me and Kimora haven't had sex yet, but we didn't need to. When you felt a connection to somebody, it had to be something deep. I felt like she was already mine, so I didn't need her body because I had her soul.

The only reason I had Dana with me was to soothe my heart. I didn't wanna be alone. I know that sounds like a bitch ass reason, but it's how I felt.

When we pulled up to my mother's house. I parked my whip and I got out my ride. I opened the passenger side door for Dana and held her hand as we walked to the back yard. When we got to the back, the party was jumping. My moms had it set out from the DJ to the picture man, and hella food was everywhere. A lot of family and friends were around, and everyone was dancing, laughing, and chilling.

I spotted my mother over by the food table, and I walked over and tapped her shoulder. She looked at me and smiled.

"My baby boy! I'm so happy to see you," she squealed.

I leaned in and kissed her cheeks.

"Happy birthday, Mama," I replied as I handed her a card that held some money in it.

"Thanks, son. You know you didn't have to do that."

"Whatever, ma. How are you enjoying everything?" I asked as I look around.

"It's lovely. I'm so shocked that so many people came out to help me celebrate." She was all smiles, and that's what I liked to see on my mom's face.

"Hello, Dana, how are you?"

"I'm good, Ms. Hughes. Is my mama here?" she asked.

Dana's mom and my mom went to the same church. That's how I met her ass. My mother told her yes, and she instructed her on where to find her mother., Dana kissed me on the cheek and walked off, heading toward where her mother was seated.

"You know your brother is here," my mom said as soon as Dana was out of earshot.

"Oh yeah?" I wanted to ask her, but I was glad I didn't.

As much as my brother wasn't around, my mother had a love hate relationship with him. She couldn't stand the ground he walked on sometimes.

"Yeah, and he has some young woman with him. She looks like she's been getting beat up too," she scoffed, and I shook my head. I already knew that was Kimora.

See, my mom and my brother had a bad history of domestic violence. Back in the day, he couldn't control his anger, and he used to hit my mom. I wasn't old enough back then to defend her, and by the time I was thirteen years old, he was already out the house. I'll never understand why my moms didn't call the police on him. Terror was always crazy, but I guess by him being her first born, she allowed him to get away with whatever. But I wouldn't dare raise my hand to a woman. That was coward shit to me.

"I just bet she is. You know that's Knox twin sister, though," I told her matter-of-factly.

She gasped and held her hand over her mouth.

"You've got to be kidding me. How did she end up with him?"

"Ma, I don't know," I lied.

I didn't wanna go into detail with her about that shit.

"Wow, well you need to inform Knox that his sister is way in over her head. If they know like we know, she would leave him and never look back," my mom said.

"What y'all over here yapping about?" Terror's voice came from behind us, and my mother jumped.

I hated that my mom felt some type of fear for his bitch ass.

"Nothing, son. How's everything going? Are you enjoying the party?" she asked him with a smile.

"Yeah, it's cool. Happy Birthday, *Mother.*" He smiled at her, and it was something about his smile that was sinister, and I hated it. Ole bitch ass nigga.

"Okay, well let me get back to my guests. If you boys need anything, don't hesitate to come and find me," she said and walked away.

"What's up, little brother? You still ain't thought about making that move yet?" he asked.

"Nah, I'm good, Big Homie. I don't like 60/40 money, I need all mine," I replied and walked away from him. I could hear him laughing behind me, but I didn't care.

I walked over to where some of my cousins were playing spades and decided to get in on the game. It wasn't my turn yet, so I decided to fall back until it was my time to hop on the table and bust these niggas' asses. I still haven't spotted Kimora, so I decided to look in the house for her.

When I entered the house through the kitchen, she was sitting at the island. She had make up on her face, and her long hair was curled tightly. The burgundy lipstick she wore gave her lips a pouty look. She looked sexy, but she also looked sad.

"Mora what's up?" I said, causing her to glance up at me.

"Hey… Hey, Prince," she said as she looked around.

"Who you looking for, Terror?"

"Yeah, I am. Ya brother is crazy." She chuckled nervously, saying it in a joking manner, but in all actuality, she was scared for her fucking life.

"You just now realizing that shit? He ain't got no security with him today, huh?" I looked around, noticing she was all alone.

"No, your mother wouldn't allow him to bring them inside, but they are in the car." She rolled her eyes.

"Kimora, why you doing this shit? Why you fucking with this nigga when I'm begging you to leave him alone?"

"Who is that you're with? I spotted you with ole girl when you came through the back yard," she said, ignoring my initial question.

"That's my friend, Dana," I told her honestly.

Even though Dana and I were fucking, we were only friends.

"Oh, I can't tell she's a friend, not with the way you were holding her hand."

"Really, shawty? You fucking my brother!" I spoke through gritted teeth.

"BUT I'M NOT FUCKING HIM!" she shouted.

"Shit, I can't tell. Not the way that nigga seems to have a hold on you. I'm tryna rock with you for real because I love you for you, but you straight playing a nigga. You either want me or you don't! We spent two days together! TWO!

And I haven't heard from you since. What type of shit is that?" I growled.

I was fucking pissed at her ass.

"I'm not ignoring you. I have shit to take care of, and until it's taken care of, my mind won't really be free."

"You keep talking in fucking circles. What's the fucking agenda?"

"Revenge," she spat and looked at me with coldness in her eyes.

"Revenge? Revenge on who, Terror? You think you can take this nigga down or something? I would love to know what tricks you have up your sleeve if niggas in the streets can't take him out."

"It doesn't matter. I got this. That's all you need to worry about. Don't worry about me, and don't try to love me, because I can't be loved. I'm damaged, Prince, and there's nothing no one can do to change it. I'm mentally fucked up. And I can admit that abut myself."

"You ain't mentally fucked up. You seeking something that's not worth seeking. Challenging this muthafucka can be detrimental to ya health, but you don't hear nobody talking to you. You only wanna do what you wanna do."

"What is it, Prince? You just wanna see what it's like to fuck a fat girl? Whatchu digging on me so hard for? You tryna get the pussy," she spat, and I mugged her.

"Look, man, don't ever come at me like that. I like you for you! If I didn't, I wouldn't be here right now. So, miss me with that 'cause I'm fat' shit. Every nigga don't be trying to fuck either. I ain't fucked you yet, and I love you, so what the fuck does that mean? You tryna make me out to be something that I'm not. You want me to stop fighting for you, you want me to say fuck all of this, but I ain't about to do that shit. When you vibe with a muthafucka, you just vibe, and sex ain't got a damn thing to do with it. Anybody can bust a nut, baby girl. That shit is nothing to me. I've been fucking since I was thirteen years old, so you think getting some pussy moves me? Nah, the fuck it doesn't, but you wanna be stubborn, spiteful, and revengeful, and you ain't doing shit but setting yo own ass up for failure."

"Okay, I'm done with the fucking lecture," she sassed then placed her Gucci shades on her face and tossed her long hair toward her back.

I chuckled. I guess she was full of herself now. Fuck out of here.

"You mean to tell me you will be able to live with yourself if something happens to Jessica?" I questioned.

The smug look she gave me washed off her face and was replaced by a look of sadness.

"I know you won't. When Terror came into her home and violated her in the worst way, you should've bailed on his ass then, but nah, you walking around this muthafucka with this nigga talm about you got an agenda. Fuck yo agenda! Why don't you think about the other people in your life that you putting in yo bullshit? Knox was ready to kill everything fucking moving for you, yet you still don't care. Get out yo feelings, Kimora, and let it go. Get the fuck away from the nigga. If you don't want me, then cool, I'll fall back. But get the fuck away from Terror," I told her and walked away.

I didn't have time for her confused, crazy ass. She was

right. She was mentally fucked up, and I couldn't fix her problems. When I made it outside, I found Dana talking to one of my oldest cousins.

"Hey baby, is everything alright?" she asked, and I let out a deep sigh.

"It will be. What's up, though? What y'all doing over here?" I asked, trying to remain normal, but no lie, I was hot.

Kimora had pissed me the fuck off because she was being stupid as fuck right now.

I engaged in conversation with Dana and my cousin, and out the corner of my eye, I spotted Kimora coming out of the house. She walked up to Terror, and I couldn't take my eyes off them. Some words were exchanged, and he smacked the shit out of her in front of everybody in the yard.

"Yo! What the fuck!" I shouted as I ran over to them and threw a right hook to Terror's face.

He stumbled backward and tried to rush me, but his old ass couldn't keep up. I threw blow after blow until his bitch ass was on the ground. I beat the shit out of my brother. I was sick and tired of him, and if he wasn't in my mother's backyard, I would've blew his fucking brains out of his head. Bitch ass nigga.

Two of my male cousins pulled me off him, but not without me getting one last kick off of him.

"Let me the fuck go!" I shouted, and I looked around and my mother had tears in her eyes.

Everyone was standing around and staring at me, but I didn't give any fucks. I wanted to kill that bitch ass nigga. I was falling for Kimora, and I had a loyalty to Knox. I needed to protect her from harm, and I didn't give a fuck if it was my brother. That nigga was evil as hell.

Terror stood up with blood and shit dripping from his head, and his mouth was leaking, but he looked at me and laughed uncontrollably, and I knew then that this nigga was sick.

"That's how ya do yo old man, son?" he asked me, and I was confused.

"Nigga, what the fuck you talking about?" I shouted.

"I'm talking to my one and only son. Tell him, Patricia, who the fuck I am! I ain't ya fucking brother and never was!" he said, looking at my moms, and she hung her head.

"Wait... What the fuck is he talking about, ma?"

I was confused as fuck. This some sick ass shit if this is true.

"Princeton..."

"Is it true, Ma?" I whispered as I walked up on her.

"Princeton..."

"IS IT TRUE?" I yelled as spittle flew from my mouth.

"Yes," she said in a low tone, and I shook my head.

Tears formed in my eyes, and I didn't wanna cry in front of everybody. I left of the backyard in haste. I hopped in my ride and peeled off. Shit was embarrassing as fuck, and I knew I was never gonna speak to my mother again. I didn't even wanna know how or why this shit happened.

If this nigga Terror is my fucking father, then why would she lie to me all these years saying, he was my brother. I didn't know what type of sick shit was going the fuck on with my moms, but I knew I would never be the same after this shit.

TRUTH IS

SPIRIT

I walked back into the club, and all eyes were on me as I went to the dressing rooms. I swore that I wouldn't set foot back into this club, but after Knox's crazy ass side chick or whoever the fuck she was bust my living room windows out, I knew then I couldn't fuck with him. She put my tires on flat and that was it for me.

I wouldn't be able to survive fucking with this chick. For it to only be sex, she was surely obsessed. I thought my ex, Tyree had a damn problem, but this chick was truly something special. I couldn't take it.

Knox called me all day every day, and I hadn't answered not one time for him. I was weak for him, and he knew it. As much as I wanted to tell myself that I didn't like Knox like that, I couldn't because I was low key falling in love with him. It was just something about him.

But after that fiasco, I wanted nothing else to do with him. The chick could have him. He wasn't worth the drama. I had enough shit going on in my life.

"What's up, sis? You back in the building?" Cream smiled when saw me, and I slightly rolled my eyes.

"Yes, I'm here, girl," I took a deep sigh and walked into my dressing room.

The owner, Clarence, never gave it to another girl. I've only been gone for two weeks. I was sort of depressed after the situation with Knox and ole girl, so I needed a breather from everybody. I just didn't wanna work, but those bills started piling up on me, so I was back now because I have to do what I gotta do.

I sat at my vanity and stared at myself in the mirror. Tears formed in my eyes, and I couldn't help but to cry. I couldn't believe I was back at this shit hole. I started to sob as I thought about everything that I was going through at the moment, and before I knew it, I was trashing my dressing room. I knocked all the perfumes off, the jewelry, boas, costumes, everything. I was sick and tired of being sick and tired. I just wanted it all to fucking end.

I finally caught my breath as I stared at myself in the mirror, and I was a wreck. I had a secret that was eating me alive, and I didn't know how I would be able to live with myself. I felt like shit for doing what I did. I couldn't tell a soul, though, because no one would understand my logic. No one would understand the reason I made my decision.

"Desire?" Cream knocked on my dressing room door.

"Yeah girl," I shouted, and she came inside.

"Girl, you got some fine ass chocolate specimen waiting

out front for you." She smiled, and my heart rate increased. I knew she had to be talking about Knox.

"Okay," I replied trying not to show my fear. He had an tendency to be a little off if you ask me.

"Wait.... what the hell happened in here? It looks like a tornado been through here," she said, observing the mess that I had made.

"Girl, nothing. I got frustrated looking for something that's all." I chuckled, trying to play it off. But, in reality, I had a mental fucking breakdown.

"Oh okay, well yeah, the cutie is up in the front asking about you." She walked off, and I exhaled.

I didn't feel like talking to Knox, but he wasn't anything like Tyree. He wasn't just gonna go away easily.

I dressed in my attire first before I headed out to see him. My nerves were rattled, and I needed a shot or something ASAP. I put on the diamond studded bra and a black thong, my black stilettos, and my hair was in a ponytail, resembling the style of a genie. I applied some gloss to my lips, and once I was dressed, I walked out of the dressing room and to the front of the club. When I got to the front, Knox was standing near the bar. I could tell he was scanning the crowd. He was paranoid like that.

When his eyes landed on me, a frown came upon his face. I sashayed over to him, and he stared me up and down. I felt so small under his stare. His eyes were intimidating, and it caused me to look away from him

"What's good, shawty?"

"Hello, Knox."

"You ain't been seeing a nigga call you?" he asked.

"I have."

"You have? Then what? Ya fucking phone don't work?" he growled, and I laughed.

"It works just fine, but I don't wanna talk to you anymore, Knox. The drama you have brought into my life so far has not been worth it at all," I told him, and he rubbed his chin while staring down at me.

"Spirit, let me tell you like this. I told you I wasn't giving up that easily when it came to you. I told you I wasn't fucking with Gianna anymore, yet you refused to believe me. I don't get you. I told you I was gonna get the window fixed, yet you sent the workers away when they came to ya house to fix the shit. I don't get you"

"I don't need shit from you, Knox. I would rather do without. I told you I wanted a man who was all mine. I don't want an *everybody nigga,* a nigga everybody done had. And on top of that, ya little girlfriend is crazy as fuck. My mother is in that house, and she's sick! That shit was uncalled for. And I don't got time for that shit."

"Fuck all that shit you spitting. My only concern is why the fuck are you back in this club? Didn't I tell you that shit was a wrap? You comfortable shaking ya ass for a bunch of niggas you don't fucking know?" He was ready to spazz the fuck out.

"Chill with all of that shit. This is how I pay my bills," I retorted, and he laughed.

"Man, miss me with the dumb shit. Get ya shit and let's go, Spirit. I'm not about to be playing with yo water headed ass. The fuck," he snapped, and I laughed.

"Fuck you, Knox," I said and tried to walk off form him,

but that didn't go over well because he grabbed me back by my ponytail, and I fell to the floor. Completely embarrassed, my face was red hot with anger as I hopped up off the floor and got in his face.

"Fuck you gon' do? Walk away from me again." He grinned, and I smacked the shit out of him.

I wanted to embarrass him just as much as he embarrassed me.

"Fuck you!" I screamed, and security ran over to my aid.

"You got a problem, Desire?" the big security guard asked, calling me by my stage name.

"Nah, muthafucka, do you got a problem? Mind ya fucking business," Knox said then pulled a gun from his waistband and aimed it at the security guard's head.

My eyes bucked at the sight of the gun. I don't know how in the fuck he got a gun in the club.

"Aye, brother, it's all good. I was just checking on the lady." The guard bitched up instantly, but I would too if a big ass gun was aimed in my direction.

"Spirit, go get ya shit and hurry the fuck up," he demanded, and I complied.

The only reason why I complied is that I didn't want Knox acting a fool in the club. I went to the back and grabbed my things. I was shaking so badly. I had never seen him act like that, and I definitely didn't wanna be a witness to a fucking murder.

After grabbing my things, I headed back to the front of the club, and Knox still had his gun trained on the bouncer. When he saw me, he smiled. His crazy ass grabbed my hand and led me toward the entrance of the club.

Once we were out the club and in his car, he finally put his gun away. I looked over at him and rolled my eyes.

"You can't force me to fuck with you," I told him, and he chuckled.

"Man, you ain't going nowhere."

"If I would have tried, you probably would've tried to shoot me."

"Who you talking to, Spirit?"

"You, nigga!" I shouted. I was irritated by him

"Man, shawty, I would never do anything to fucking hurt you. You just smacked the shit out of me, and I didn't do shit. I would never put my hands back on you. I ain't built like that, shawty, but I will lay a muthafucka down for you. That's what I will do. I just want you to stop playing with me and understand when you fucking with a gangsta."

"Knox, if you think strong arming yourself into my life is gonna cut it, well newsflash, my nigga, it's not. I like you, I mean like you a whole lot, but…"

"You mean you love me? You love me, Spirit. And it's okay to say it."

"Whatever, Knox. See how rude you are, cutting me off and shit."

"My bad, shawty. But real shit. I'm tryna see where we can go with us. I'm ready to fuck with you the long way. You were supposed to been mine, but that bullshit happened with me going to the joint, so it threw everything off that was supposed to happen between us," he said, and I shook my head.

"You think you know everything?"

226

"Not everything, but something close to it," he replied as he glanced at me and winked.

"Whatever." I scoffed, rolling my eyes.

Me and Knox drove back to my house. Once inside, I called myself ignoring him, but he wouldn't allow me to. As soon as I stepped into the shower, he came in the bathroom and got in the shower with me.

We fucked in the shower, and then afterward, we fucked in the bedroom. The whole time I screamed his name and clawed his back, I couldn't help but think to myself how I really did love him. And I couldn't see him not being in my life.

WHEN IT'S ALL SAID AND DONE

KIMORA

Sitting on Terror's king-size bed, I couldn't help but think about what I had gotten myself into. I fucked up when it came to this man. He was crazy ass fuck, and at this point psychotic. He was truly a piece of work.

He wouldn't let me go home ever since he let me go back home and I disappeared again and was with Prince. I knew Jessica was worried sick about me, but I kept texting and calling her to let her know that I'm fine. I hadn't spoken to Knox since I called him and let him know that I was alright I knew my brother was on a rampage looking for me, but I needed to do this shit alone, I couldn't risk him going back to jail.

Prince hadn't been responding to my text messages. I couldn't believe Terror was his father. I didn't understand how. I didn't know what Prince's mom had going on, but that was some freaky shit. And now it felt even worse that I was fucking with Prince's daddy instead of his brother. I knew Prince was pissed at me, but he didn't see the bigger the picture. No one did. I was driven by hate in my heart. I wanted the nigga to suffer so fucking bad. He was beating my ass, but it would all be worth it in the end. I've gotten close to him for a reason.

"Please... Please... Terror!" I heard a woman's voice cry out from downstairs.

That broke my train of thought, and I got out of the bed and went to see what was going on. As I went down the stairs toward where I heard the voices, the sounds of the woman crying broke my heart.

I entered the living room where Terror and his men were standing around in a circle. My heart rate increased at the sight of the lady in front of me. I vowed to never see this bitch again.

"Good morning, sweetheart" Terror smiled, coming to stand next to me.

He kissed me on the cheek, but my focus wasn't on him. It was on Candice. My step mother, she was bloody and badly beaten. I looked around for her son, Trey, and he was nowhere around, which was surprising because he was always with Terror's crew.

"Good morning," I replied in a low tone as I looked down at Candice bawling her eyes out.

I didn't know what the fuck was going on, but this bitch, the bitch who made my life a living fucking hell, the bitch who caused damn near all my pain. I felt nothing for her as I looked at her battered and bruised body. I swear I hated this bitch.

"You see, sweetheart, what happens when you're not loyal?" he snickered, circling Candice.

"I'm sorry, Terror. I promise I'm gonna come up with your money. Just give me a ch… chance," she begged him, and I couldn't help but smirk.

I couldn't help it. The evilness that crept in my soul was a feeling I've never felt before. I was happy as fuck to see this bitch on her knees begging for her life.

"Ki… Kimora…" she said my name, and I squinted at her.

"Don't ever say my name from ya filthy fucking lips," I snarled and then did something that I've wanted to do for so long.

I kicked the fuck out of her ass as if she was a dog laying on the streets.

"Ohhhhhhh weeee!!! I like that feisty shit!" Terror cackled.

"Do you love me, Kimora?" he asked me, and it felt weird because the question came out of nowhere,

"What?" I asked, mind boggled.

I didn't love him. In fact, I hated him just as much as I hated Candice. Actually, I hated him more.

"You heard me." He smirked. "Do you love me Kimora?" he asked again, but I didn't respond.

Instead, I put my focus on Candice.

"Are you gonna kill this bitch or what?" I snarled.

"I wasn't, but you can," he stated and handed me his gun out of his waist band.

I was more confused. I had never hurt anyone, let alone killed them. So, I was scared, confused, and full of anger. I didn't take the gun from him because I didn't want to do it. As much as I hatred Candice, as much as I felt like she had wronged me, I couldn't do it.

"Take the fucking gun!" he barked at me, and I looked at him.

My hands shook with nervousness as I reached out and grabbed the gun from his hands.

"Pleaseeee don't do this... Please... I'm sorry for everything I've ever done..." she begged, and my heart rate increased.

I still held aim on the gun, but I couldn't pull the trigger for nothing in the world. I guess I was taking too long for Candice.

"Do it sweetheart and I'm not gonna say it again" Terror growled

"She's a weak bitch! She can't do it!" Candice said.

"If you're gonna do it, then do it you fat bitch..." she growled as the tears streamed down her face.

She turned into a different person right before my eyes. I was confused, and I cocked my head to the side as I stared at her.

"I said do it then you scary bitch. You ain't shit, and never was. You'll always be a fat, scary, sloppy, bitch! Just like ya father ain't shit...." She growled, and my demeanor switched up cold on her.

In that instant, I pulled the trigger, three times, hitting her twice in the chest and once in the stomach. When her body fell over, I dropped the gun and ran up the stairs to

Terror's bedroom, where I bawled my eyes out across the bed until I cried myself to sleep.

SOMETHING BEING THROWN ON ME WOKE ME UP OUT OF MY sleep. I sat up in bed and was startled by the liquid, the smell of what it was finally hit me, and I was confused. It was rubbing alcohol. I frowned and looked around, and Terror was sitting in a chair near the bed

"Sleep well?' he asked me with a smirk on his face.

He had a box of matches in his hands and flicked one by one, blowing them out while talking to me.

"Have you ever been burned?" he asked me, and my nerves got rattled all over the place.

"What? What's wrong?" I asked him confused.

"Have you ever been burned? Answer the question, Kimora." He grinned, and an eerie feeling crept up on me.

"No."

"Do you wanna see what it's like to be burned alive?" he asked me

"No." I trembled as tears fell from my eyes.

"Then the next time I ask you if you love me or not, answer the muthafucking question. You embarrassed me in front of my men, and I cannot have that. My respect is everything, sweetheart. Do you understand me?" he asked and flicked one more match, letting the fire linger on top of it.

"I understand"

"Good. Now clean up and get ready. We have a dinner

date with some of my business associates," he said and blew out the fire from the last match.

He then got up and walked out of the room. I trembled with fear as I was afraid to move. I knew I had to heed the warning because I was literally fucking with fire dealing with Terror. I had end his existence and ASAP.

I got out the bed and took a shower as I showered I thought about all the ways I could kill him. After showering, I got dressed and met him in the foyer. I was dressed in a gold sequined dress and some gold stilettos. The dress hugged my curves like never before, and I was digging it. Too bad it was worn to go out with a psycho.

Me and Terror went out to dinner with some Columbian guys. I guess they were his connects, or he was thinking about snaking his old connects. I wasn't really paying attention to the conversation. My thoughts were on Prince and how I missed him. How I wanted to talk to him and kiss him. I knew he was pissed at me for doing what the fuck I was doing, but my heart wouldn't rest until I felt some type of gratification.

Once we made it back to the mansion, Terror was in rare form. He had been drinking, and he only got worse. His mouth was off the chain, and his demands were beyond ridiculous. He was a sick piece of shit who needed to be put down a long fucking time ago.

As I got undressed in the bedroom, I spotted the gun he had me kill Candice with earlier lying on top of the dresser. Terror was in the bathroom, and I took that as my cue to grab the gun. This was my opportunity to end it all.

I waited until he came out the bathroom, and when he did, I aimed the gun in his direction.

"Whoa, whoa, sweetheart. What's this all about?" He grinned.

I wasn't about to do all this talking, but I did need to let him know the reason he was dying.

"Fuck you! You evil son of a bitch!" I screamed, and he laughed.

"I knew you were a killa. I guess you weren't some punk ass bitch"

"Fuck you! I hate you, muthafucka! You ruined my life!" I shouted as tears came to my eyes.

I was trying to be tough as nails, but my emotions were pouring out. I'd been through so much shit, and to think that this was finally over had me all over the place.

"Ruined your life?" He laughed.

"You killed my father! I was home that day you did it! I would never forget your voice!" I screamed as tears poured out of my eyes.

It was true, I would never forget how he was so fucking cold toward my daddy as he begged and pleaded for his life.

"I've killed many men, baby girl, be more specific." He folded his arms across his chiseled, bare chest. He thought this was a game, he thought this was a joke.

"Captain Louis Eldredge! That was my father! So that's why you killed my little brother, Kade, because he knew what you did! He knew you killed our father," I cried.

"No, I killed that fucker because he was talking to the feds," he growled.

I mugged his ass. Nisa didn't tell me that Kade was talking to the feds.

"I don't care why you did it, but you have to die now. You took away two people that I love in the whole fucking world. You took away my soul when you killed my daddy."

"That muthafucka was already dying. Do you know how good it felt to see the good ole captain brought down to his knees?" he smirked as he walked closer to me.

My hands shook with nervousness as he walked up on me. The gun was touching his chest. He was so close to me, I felt like I couldn't breathe. I was scared as hell.

See, Nisa told me that Kade said if anything ever happened to him to call Kimora and tell her that Terror did it. He knew he wouldn't be around for too much longer. He knew Terror killed our Daddy because he had the nerve to brag about it. Also, the bitch Candice set my father up and lied about it.

The moment I heard Terror's voice at the repast, I knew it was all too familiar. He was the one who broke into my house and ordered his men to kill my father, and with Nisa's confirmation from Kade, I vowed I was gonna take his ass out.

When I killed Candice, I knew what she did, but I still felt some sort of sympathy for her. After she talked jazzy at the mouth, it was nothing for me to pull the trigger.

"The good ole Captain Louis. He denied my entrance into the military! He felt I wasn't good enough, well look at how life would have it! He wasn't fucking good enough. He was weak! A fucking dope fiend. The captain was part of the reason I became a drug dealer, and look at how karma would play out in his life. He was at my doorstep beggin' for drugs. He stooped to the bottom of the gutter. He wasn't an honorable man like the media and newspapers claimed he was, he was a weak, worthless piece of shit. And you're just like him, sweetheart.

"Nothing about you stands for honor Why do you think I degraded you so much? You didn't think I knew he was ya father? I knew exactly who you were as well as Kade. These are my fucking streets, and I know everyone in them. How did it feel to watch ya daddy suck on a glass dick? Or better yet, how did it feel to watch your father gurgle on his blood?" he said in a low tone, and as tears raced out of my eyes, my vision became blurry.

Shoot him, Kimora, I coached myself.

"You oughta be grateful for life because I had plans to kill you, but I fell in love with you, and now you can't ever leave me, sweetheart. You're my sweetheart, and I own you. You still have to pay off ya father's debt. He was never paid in full before he left this earth."

When he said that, I squeezed the trigger. *Click, click, click,* nothing happened. There weren't any bullets in the gun. Terror looked at me with a grin etched on his face, and then he smacked the shit out of me, causing me to fall to the ground. The gun fell from my hands, and then he punched me on the side of my face, causing me to go dizzy.

I looked around and spotted my stiletto shoe out the corner of my eye. I grabbed it up in a hurry and stabbed the heel into his dick.

"Ooowwwww fuck! You stupid bitch!" he growled as he stumbled backward.

I got off the floor and raced out of the bedroom and down the stairs. I spotted my car keys hanging in the hook and grabbed them up. This shit was over. I was telling Knox ASAP because I knew Terror wasn't gonna stop coming for me. I should've killed him, but I didn't have anything to do it with. I had to get away and fast. I raced out of his front door, flying past the guards who wore confusion on their faces, and hopped in my ride, I started my ignition and peeled away, crying the entire time.

WHAT THE HELL?

SPIRIT

"Yes, ma'am; your five weeks pregnant," the doctor told me, and I sat up in shock.

I was so busy being with Knox that I hadn't stopped to realize that I haven't seen my period. I swallowed hard as the doctors gave me all types of prescriptions and prenatal pills. I couldn't even function right now.

I didn't know how I was gonna tell him about the baby, but I knew I couldn't. I couldn't have a baby right now. That wasn't in my plans.

I walked out of the doctor's office with my heart racing. I wanted to cry so bad, but I held the shit in. Instead of going back to Knox's place, I drove to the nail salon. Maybe if I pampered myself, I would feel a little bit better.

Pulling up to the nail salon, I exhaled deeply as I got out

my ride. I walked past the barber shop that was connected to it, and a bunch of guys were standing outside around it.

"What's good, gorgeous?" a nigga spoke to me, but I ignored his ass.

"Yo, bruh, that's Desire for that strip club Infatuation," his home boy said.

I swear that shit aggravated me. Those were the times I hated being a stripper.

"Come and make it clap for a nigga, I got a couple of dollars," the nigga said, and I turned around and glared at him.

"Ya money ain't long enough, fuck boy," I snapped.

I was sick of these dog ass niggas out here.

"Bitch, who…"

"Aye, dog, watch ya fucking mouth," a voice said, coming out of the beauty salon.

I turned around and Tyree was standing there. He was still fine as hell to me, but I didn't love him anymore.

They looked at Tyree but didn't say shit. They just resumed their conversation as if nothing just happened. Tyree strolled over to me with a grin on his face.

"What's up, Spirit? How you been ma?" he asked.

"I'm good, just going to get my nails done." I smiled.

"That's good, you still looking like a snack outchea and shit," he joked.

"I try, I try. But how been though?"

"I'm maintaining. Shit a nigga just getting a cut."

"Oh okay. Well it was good seeing you Tyree," I said and tried to walk off, but he stopped me.

"Let me ask you something. Is that nigga treating you right?"

"He is, I'm happy."

"But he ain't me, though."

"He's not, and that's a good thing Tyree." I laughed, and he smirked

"I fucked up with you, Spirit, but know that I'll always have love for you, ma," he spoke.

"I know, Tyree, I feel the same." I kissed his cheek and walked away.

What me and Tyree had was something neither of us could explain. He was my first real love, real relationship, or anything like that. He just didn't know how to treat me, better yet he couldn't keep his dick in his pants.

Knox valued the type of woman I was. He loved me, and he showed me in every way possible, even though at times he pissed me off because he still had no control over the crazy bitch. Somehow the bitch got my number and she's been calling and playing on my phone, and I was sick of that shit with her ass.

As I sat down at the pedicure bowl, I pulled out my phone and saw that I had three text messages from Knox.

My King: who the fuck you kissing on the cheek Spirit?

My King: you want me to pull up on you? Why you ain't responding?'

My King: Spirit!

I immediately called him back because I didn't need that type of drama. I looked outside and that's when I spotted his friend Benz walking to his car. He had to have been the person to call and tell him that shit. Damn, if it wasn't one thing it's another.

"Yo," he answered on the first ring.

"Knox, what are you talking about?" I asked in a low tone.

I didn't need for everyone in this damn shop to hear my fucking business.

"Man, you know what the fuck I'm talking about. You out there chatting it up with niggas and shit."

"Tell Benz why the fuck he in my business. I can have a causal conversation. I'm not fucking nobody. Damn, why you calling me with the drama, Knox? I'm not in the fucking mood for that shit," I snapped at him.

"Benz?"

"Yeah Benz, I saw that nigga," I spat, and Knox laughed.

"Man, chill out. I just want you to know that I'm always watching yo ass." He chuckled, and I rolled my eyes.

"Spirit," he called out my name, but I didn't respond.

"Spirit..."

"Yes?"

"I'm sorry, aight."

"Alright..." I exhaled.

"Nah man, real shit. I'm sorry, bae. Whatchu doing when you leave the nail shop?" he asked, trying to switch up the conversation.

"I'm going home, I need to relieve the nurse. And I miss my momma, so I'm going to spend some time with her," I told him.

"Aight man, hit me when you leaving the nail shop so I can know you made it home safely," He instructed me.

"Okay, bae... will do." I hung up the phone and closed my eyes as the nail tech worked on my feet.

After finishing my spa day, I was finally headed home. Before I made it to the crib, I stopped at the soul food restaurant and got me and my moms something to eat. As I drove home, Knox called me back.

"Heyy, babe," I answered.

"Where you at?"

"I'm pulling up to my house right now," I told him as I parked my car in front of the driveway.

I tucked the phone underneath my ear and grabbed the bags out the backseat.

"I thought I told you to call me when you were on your way home," he snapped, and I giggled.

"I'm sorry, Knox...Okay..."

"Aight man, I'll be over there in a minute. I'm handling some business right now."

"Okay, Bae..."

"Yo birthday next week, whatchu trying to do?"

"I don't know I wanted to do a baecation though, maybe Vegas or Miami. I'm not sure yet," I told him as I stuck the key in the door.

I still hadn't figured out how I was gonna tell him that I was pregnant.

"Oh, that's cool. It's whatever you wanna do, ma. It's yo day," he said, and I smiled.

Since he was in a good mood, I figured now would be a good time to tell him that I'm pregnant.

"Bae... I got something to tell you."

"What, man?"

"I'm..."

The words didn't flow from my mouth because the sight before my eyes caused me to drop the phone to the floor as tears rushed to the forefront of my eyes. Sitting on my living room couch was Knox's crazy ass ex Gianna, she was holding a gun to my mother's head and smiling while staring at me.

"Welcome home, beautiful."

I THINK I LOVE HER

PRINCE

"Bae, you need to get up and go talk to your mother," Dana said, coming into the bedroom.

She was clad in her panties and bra, and I was still in my boxers.

It had been two weeks since that fiasco with Terror and Kimora at Mom's barbeque, and I had no words for anyone. I was sick to my stomach. I didn't know all the details, and in fact, I didn't wanna know. I wanted to forget all this shit happened for a reason. I was sick and fucking tried of the bullshit, the lies, and the secrets.

"I don't got shit to say to her."

"And why don't you?"

"Because I fucking don't! Leave me the fuck alone about it"

"Well you need to get ya mind right, you ain't fucked me

since that day. I'm horny, and every time I approach you, you push me away like shit I'm not worth anything to you."

"You're not!" I snapped but I didn't mean it.

"What?"

"Ohhh, I get it, it's the fat bitch you love, right? The one you hit ya daddy over right? I saw the way you looked at her. If that's who you want, then say that shit! Stop stringing me along because I don't have time for it Prince."

"Man, fuck this."

I was irritated by Dana and her chattering in my ear. I just wanted to be left the fuck alone. I got up off the bed and placed my clothes on my body. I grabbed my car keys and headed for the door.

"Where you going, Prince? You just gonna walk away? Prince!" she shouted my name, but I ignored her as I kept moving toward my ride.

When I got in my car I exhaled deeply and then started my ignition. I didn't feel like being bothered with anybody, as I drove my cell chimed and it was a message from my mother.

Please call me son, it read and as mad as I was to her I knew I had to talk to my mom's. I loved my mother too much to not talk to her in forever. So I bit the bullet and called her.

"Yeah," I said into the phone

"Princeton...can we talk. It's a lot you don't understand" she said in a hushed voice.

"We can, where are you?" I asked

"I'm Visiting Princess" she said and I swallowed hard.

"Okay....meet me at the restaurant"

"Are you gonna come and see her?" she asked me and I didn't know how to answer that

"Not right now. I just saw her last week."

"This is a different week."

"I know, Mom."

"Okay, I'll meet you at Applebee's right now," she stated and hung up the phone.

I headed toward Applebee's on 95th and western. Me and my Momma needed to have this major sit down. I needed answers and asap.

When I got the restaurant I was seated at a booth. I waited patiently for my mom to come. As I sat there I received a text message form Kimora, and I just looked at it, I didn't even respond because I honestly had nothing to say to her either. I was tired f fighting for her. She wanted to deal with that nigga Terror then so be it. Fuck her.

My momma waltzed in moments later and she wore a big smile on her face. Her eyes looked tired and I didn't feel bad. I wasn't the one who lied to her all these years she lied to me.

"Hello, son." She kissed me on the cheek.

"Hey, ma." She took a seat across from me and we both stared at each other without saying anything.

"Okay son I don't know how to begin with this..." She shook her head as tears clouded the rim of her eyes.

"Just spit out. It ain't that hard. "

"But it is Princeton!"

"How is he my father! But you've been telling me all these years that he's my brother? Its sick and I want to know why? Why momma?' I asked her as my voice cracked. The tears rolled down her cheeks, as she began to speak.

"Princeton, when I was 20 years old I met a man Name Donald Bash, he was the love of my life, and I wanted nothing more in this world then to give him a baby. But I never could, so when we married I was 22 years old and I felt like I was getting older and I still hadn't conceived. We ended up adopting ab child. Jamie was 10 years old when we got him. I wanted a newborn, but Donald felt like Jamie was the perfect age to groom, but what he didn't know what that Jamie had a dark soul.

"He used to torture the animals in the neighborhood, beat up all the little boys, touch the girls underneath their skirts, just making a mockery of us as his parents. But all in all, we tried to love him like parents should. Even when I wanted to give up Donald wouldn't. He had hope for Jamie. Well the day of my 26th birthday, Donald had went out to the supermarket to get some things for my birthday dinner, but he never made it back home. He was killed by a drunk driver. That was the day my heart was broken into pieces, I was never the same, and neither was Jamie. When we lost Donald, that took a little bit of both of us."

"Wait so he was adopted?"

"Yes, son."

"So that's still not telling me how he ended up as my father."

"Will you just listen Princeton! I'm not done talking," she snapped, and I only nodded my head. But her story was frustrating me shit sounded like a lifetime movie gone wrong.

"Jamie has always been a hothead, I took him to get evaluated when he was 14 years old because I just didn't understand how he was acting out, and the psychiatrist diagnosed him with *Impulse Control Disorder*. It's a disorder where a person is repeatedly unable to resist the sudden, forceful urge to do something that may cause self-harm or harm others. Well when he was 17 years old and I was 34 years old. He tried to enlist in the military. They denied his application because if his mental illness, and he came home irate." She shook her head as the tears flowed from her eyes. My heartbeat increased rapidly.

"He…. He raped me……and I feel so sick to my stomach every time I think about it because I allowed him to still be in my life. All of the church members knew him as my son. When I found out I was pregnant I refused to have the baby but when I saw the sonogram of you I knew without a doubt I had to keep you no matter how you got conceived, you were my first pregnancy. My baby I wanted to carry on my own for so many years," she said and my tears started to flow. That bitch ass nigga raped my mom's. He raped my fucking mother. I was fuming inside but I didn't want it to show to her.

"Princeton; do not go after Jamie, he's not sane at all. His day will come when he has to pay for all the horrible things he's done in life. I'm sorry I ever lied to you, but I didn't want you to be hurt, but I hurt you anyways. And I'm sorry son…. I'm so sorry," she cried, and I took my thumbs and wiped away her tears.

"I'm sorry too momma. I love you and no matter what happened in the past, I'm here." I said, and she smiled at me.

She excused herself, so she could go and wipe her face. I pulled out my phone and I texted Kimora back. I knew if I needed to talk I could talk to her. She told me she was out in Kankakee Illinois, and I was confused on what she was doing all the way out there, but I let her know when I finished lunch with my mom I will be out there to see her.

My head was truly fucked up now from my mom's story. I didn't care who Terror was, he had to die., for raping my mother, for beating on Kimora, for making my life a living hell. All the hurt he has caused needed to be answer too.

AFTER EATING LUNCH WITH MY MOM'S. I GOT STRAIGHT ON THE high way and headed to Kankakee, it was 45 minutes away from the city. I needed to see her, to hear her voice, I wanted to see her smile. I missed Kimora and I wasn't scared to admit it.

When I pulled up to the small house that she gave me the address to I was a bit confused on who house it was. It was small and had vines around it, with a small rose garden in the front of it. I got out of my ride and walked to the door, she peeked out the curtains before I even had a chance to knock on the door

The door swung open and Kimora was dressed in a blue sundress and her long hair was pushed up into a bun on the top of her head. She had a black eye that looked as if it was healing, and I frowned my face when I saw her. The look on her face was soft with shock and love written on it. She missed a nigga I could tell.

"Whatchu standing there for? You ain't gon come inside?" she asked me, and I nodded my head. As soon as I stepped inside the smell of vanilla and cinnamon was in the air. She closed her front door and threw her arms around my neck.

"I missed you so much" she whispered. I inhaled her scent and I wrapped my arms around her waist hugging her tightly.

"I missed you too beautiful" she took a step back and stared me up and down.

"Are you okay?" she asked me

"Shit I should be asking you that, you the one with the black eye,"

"Oh this? This is nothing but a lil war wound." She chuckled, but I wasn't feeling that.

"Nah, that's not what it looks like but we ain't gonna go there," I said as she grabbed my hand and led me to her bedroom. I walked in the bedroom and it was nice.

"Whose crib is this?" I had to ask

"Uhh, mine." She laughed

"Straight up? When you get this?"

"I've been had it since I first got my daddy's money. It was supposed to be my living residence, but I couldn't fathom leaving Jessica alone, so I just paid the rent every month, and I come by from time to time to keep up the maintenance."

"Well its dope it fits you"

"Thanks babe," she smiled.

"You alright?" she made me ask. She was too damn giddy for me.

"I'm okay'

"Where's terror?" I asked her trying to see where her head was at.

"I guess back in the city, we had a fight and I tried to kill him, but I failed. I had to run because I... I knew he was gonna come looking for me," she said, and I instantly began to Panic.

"Yo, what the fuck? Where the fuck is Jessica?" I barked because I knew he would be coming for her.

"She's okay, and she's safe. Believe me, she's safe Prince," she tried to reassure me.

"Damn! What the fuck is going on, Kimora! Why the fuck is you playing with that man! You should've killed him if you had the opportunity. You don't let a nigga like Terror live! You just don't!" I snapped on her ass.

"Please.... don't lecture me right now.... I just—"

"You just what? Don't wanna hear it? I ain't lecturing you, I'm telling you what's real."

"Just fucking kiss me already Prince. I've missed you too much. I'm tired fighting my feelings for you. I'm tired of it all. I've been out here for two weeks, and I've had time to think. I've had time to reflect on the things I did, and I see it wasn't worth it all. I did too much. My mind was on revenge, but my heart was in another place. I had too much to lose even though I had lost a lot I still had something to lose. I didn't think about Knox, Jessica, or You when I was dealing with Terror. And I'm glad I'm done with it. I'm glad its over"

"But it ain't over Kimora, he ain't gon stop until you dead and in the fucking ground ma"

"Well if its my time to go then it's my time,"

"Man, don't say no dumb shit to me like that" I snarled, and she giggled

"I'm sorry Prince, but for now can I just enjoy the time I have with you" she looked me in the eyes and I kissed her lips deeply. They felt so good against my lips. I stuck my tongue in her mouth and we tongues kissed as if I was on death row and this was the last time I was gon kiss a bitch in my life.

I pushed her back on the bed and got on top of her, I pulled the spaghetti straps down and exposed her chocolate nipples, I put one of them in my mouth and suck on it gently lightly biting her nipple. Causing her to groan in pleasure, I played with the other nipple, squeezing it between my fingers, I came up for air and kissed her lips again while I snaked my hands in between her legs. I found her clit and rubbed it gently feeling her pussy getting wetter and wetter. Damn she felt right.

"Make love to me baby," she whispered and that's what I did. I fucked Kimora into a coma for the rest of the night. Her pussy was so tight and wet I had to ask her was she a virgin.

Once it was all said and done, I laid against the headboard and she was knocked out cold, sleeping peaceful and I inhaled the blunt I was smoking, and I couldn't help but to think about her. She was a fucking goddess, and I was falling for her more and more.

My cell started to vibrate on top of her nightstand and I got off the bed to answer it. When I saw who the caller was I frowned my face up. It was 3:00 in the fucking morning.

"What, nigga?" I barked into the phone.

I walked out of the bedroom with the phone pressed against my ear because I didn't wanna wake Kimora up.

"Is that how you talk to your father?' Terror's deep voice boomed.

"Nigga ya ain't my fucking daddy, you a fucking rapist."

"Oh no, son, ya moms wanted this dick just as bad as I wanted to give it to her. Now that's neither here nor there, I'm calling because I wanted to know where my bitch is? And before you say you don't know where she is, I think it's somebody you need to talk to, because if you lie, she's dead," he spat into the phone.

When he put the person on the phone, my heart sank into my stomach. I didn't say anything for a minute after hearing the voice.

"Hello?"

"Hello?

"Yeah, nigga, I'm here!" I growled.

"So, again, where's my bitch?" He chuckled

WHO CAN I RUN TO?

KIMORA

The tapping on my leg was irritating as I sat up and opened my eyes. I didn't understand what the fuck was going on, but when I did, I thought my eyes were playing tricks on me.

"Rise and shine, sleeping beauty," Terror's deep voice rang out.

I looked around, and about six of his men were standing in my bedroom, and I was asshole naked. My eyes scanned the room looking for Prince, and I didn't see him.

"What?"

"Get the fuck out of my house!" I screamed as I grabbed the sheet and covered my body.

Terror pulled out his gun and aimed in my direction. "Get the fuck out of the bed, bitch."

"I don't care. Do it, muthafucka!" I shouted.

Where is Prince? Oh my god, where is he? Did they kill him? Did he hurt him? I had so many thoughts flowing through my mind that I didn't care if lived or died at the moment.

Terror cocked his gun back.

"Your wish is my command, sweetheart, but I love you too much to actually splatter ya fucking brains, so I'm not gonna tell you again to get the fuck up and let's go. I told you I own you," he spat, and I had to think about Knox and Jessica. I couldn't let my brother bury me. He would lose himself out here.

I slowly slid out of the bed and put my clothes on. His guard's watched me with lust filled eyes as I got dressed. I started to cry because I knew this wasn't over, but I thought I had time to run. I never would have imagined he would catch me this fast.

Once I was dressed, I was led out of my bedroom and into the living room, where Prince was sitting on the couch confused and in a daze. I looked at him, and I was confused.

"You gave me up! How could you? I thought you loved me! How could you do me like this?" I screamed as I tried to attack him, but one of Terror's goons grabbed me.

"I'm sorry, Mora," he said with his head hung.

"Look at me, muthafucka!" I screamed as tears fell from my eyes

"I'm fucking sorry! I had to! I had to!" he cried, but I wasn't hearing him. Fuck Prince and everything he stood for. He didn't love me. He was against me.

"Fuck you! Fuck you!" I screamed as I was led out of my house and placed in the back seat of Terror's ride.

When Terror got in the back seat with me, he looked at me and grinned.

"Did you ever think you could walk away from me, sweetheart? You gon' always be my bitch! And since you gave up my pussy, I'm gonna punish your pretty ass like never before," he said and punched me near my temple, causing me to black out.

To Be Continued

Never read a Bianca Marie Book?
What are you waiting for? All of the titles are available for
purchase on Amazon today!!

<u>Here's my Catalogue</u>

When Loving You Is A Crime 1: When Loving You Is A
Crime 2
When Loving You Is A Crime 3
Killing Me Softly With A Love So True (Standalone Novel)
Snow and Wynter: A Cold Love Affair 1
Snow and Wynter: A Cold Love Affair 2
Loving a Heartless Savage: Memoirs Of The Hustle 1
Loving a Heartless Savage: Memoirs Of The Hustle 2
Trap Kings and Hood queens; Ain't No Love Like A Hood
Love (Standalone)
Wicked and Mecca: A Snow and Wynter spin-off 1
Wicked and Mecca: A Snow and Wynter spin-off 2
Wicked and Mecca: A Snow and Wynter spin-off 3
Luving My Gangsta: A Hood Love Story 1
Luving My Gangsta: Hood Love Story 2
The Billions: Love, Honor, & Disloyalty
The Billions 2: The Reign Of A Billion's Wife.
The Billions 3: I am my Brother's Keeper
Hooked: Addicted to a Supreme Love
Hooked: Addicted to a Supreme Love 2
Hooked: Addicted to a Supreme Love 3
Hooked: Addicted to a Supreme Love 4

Mesmerized: The Best Love Comes From a Thug 1
Mesmerized: The Best Love Comes From a Thug 2

CPSIA information can be obtained
at www.ICGtesting.com
Printed in the USA
LVHW031724081218
599771LV00001B/33/P

9 781728 749501